BETWEEN TWO SHORES

BETWEEN TWO SHORES

Addea D. Steele

Combray House

For my parents,
Vincenza DePerno and Louis Dontino,
With love and gratitude...
May we meet again

PROLOGUE

The Confession
Tieni i tuoi amici accanto a te
(Keep your friends near to you)

Alex retreated to her childhood home with the over-powering, pungent air from the viewing room hanging in her hair and sticking to her like death itself. Stripping off her clothes, she stood under the hot shower hoping the pain and anger she felt would travel down the drain with the pelting water. Exhausted, she just wanted to sleep to escape the splitting headache that was crawling up the back of her neck.

Dried off and wrapped in the pink terry robe she'd left from her youth at her mom's house, Alex thanked God her Aunt Anna had agreed to stay for the night to watch over Christopher while she dealt with the funeral.

Luckily Chris is getting some well-deserved family time...warms my heart... has a few days to connect with my mom, along with my Aunt Anna and her son, Anthony...It's getting late...boys must already be sleeping...hmm, I don't want to wake them...tiptoe into their bedroom...ouch...step on mini car...boys...but, sweet...Chris and Anthony curled up in their matching bunk beds.

Lightly kissing Chris' forehead, she said a mother's prayer and quietly closed the door.

Alex felt some comfort snuggled up in her childhood bed. She needed the cocoon of her wistful youthful memories to get her through the night. She returned from Ricci's funeral, not only exhausted, but feeling terribly unsettled. The stress of seeing the man she hated lying dead hadn't given her the relief she'd anticipated.

All this time, I wished him dead for killing my husband...seeing him lying cold in a coffin didn't bring the satisfaction I'd expected, but it did bring painful clarity that he's ruined my life.

Once settled in with a double dose of Advil, she laid in bed thinking about the past year. Attempting to heal from Jake's death, she'd hibernated with Chris at Villa D'Oro.

Looking back, I made the right choice....withdrawing...time was what we both needed to mend our hearts...to accept Jake was gone. Retreating to our Miami home...much-needed time...healing...we're doing okay.

She'd isolated herself from Phillip, too. He tried so many times to offer a shoulder to cry on, but Alex had put him off. She saw him for the first time, in almost a year, earlier that day at the funeral.

It was so good to see him...even if it was at his father's funeral...I really did miss him all these months. He isn't to blame for Jake's death...I just couldn't deal with him...especially...since I believe his father killed Jake. What was all that about having to talk to me? That was so strange and so unlike him. I'll call him in the morning...as promised...find out what's so important soon enough.

Finally feeling groggy, she slowly drifted off to sleep. Just like every other night, her last thoughts were of Jake.

Am I imagining him next to me? This seems so real...can almost feel his warmth...I long for his touch. Some nights...I can hear him calling me...he appears in my dreams...for just a few moments, we have each other again.

Those were the dreams she didn't want to wake from.

Morning came quickly. No one needed an alarm clock with Chris and Anthony in the house. Those two little characters could get away with anything and everything with Anna and Alex's mother, Valentina. Sun was barely breaking through Alex's window when she woke from the clamor of their cheerful voices chattering outside her door. They'd already popped out of bed and were playing a game of hide and go seek with more energy than she'd had in weeks.

Breakfast at her mom's was always an occasion, especially with "Little Lord Fauntleroy," as Alex called Chris when he was at Nanna's. Valentina pulled out all the stops and relished in pampering her grandson.

Hmmm, what a way to greet the morning...whiffs of bacon drifting from my mother's kitchen. I'll just follow the nutty aroma of brewed coffee...yum...fluffy, scrambled eggs...even fluffier pancakes.

Chris and Anthony made it to the breakfast table a few minutes before Alex. Hearing their laughter floating into the hallway, Alex stopped to listen.

I love seeing Chris so happy...definitely takes away some of the sting of yesterday's funeral. He's my priority...if he's okay, then I can manage to deal with everything else.

Just as she swallowed the last bite of her mom's mouthwatering pancakes, the phone rang.

"Good morning, Phil."

Strange. He's already calling...it's only 9 A.M.

"I was going to call you soon. We just finished one of my mother's amazing breakfasts. Aunt Anna is here with Anthony, so it was a feast."

"I sure miss those mornings, Alex. I can taste your mom's famous pancakes from here. Listen, about last night. I need to talk to you, but first I have to get through my obligations today. The funeral mass is this morning and then the burial. I've decided not to host a lunch after the burial. There must have been a hundred people at my house last night. You're lucky you didn't come. I'll be free around four o'clock. Do you think you could meet me at the lake?"

"The lake, Phil? That's a forty-five-minute drive. What's wrong with meeting at your house, or better yet, why don't you just come here?"

"Alex, I need to see you alone. Please, just meet me at the lake."

"Fine. I'll be there. This better be good, Phil."

Valentina left for Ricci's funeral mass, leaving Alex a few precious hours to enjoy her aunt and the boys. Listening to their good-natured laughter reminded her of how it used to be when Jake was alive. There was always laughter in the house.

It's time to shake out of my fog...especially for Chris' sake. We've been quietly mourning long enough...not fair to him...I can see that now. He's just a boy... deserves an untroubled life. I'll always tell him stories about his dad...I promise... once we get home to Miami...things will be different.

Driving to the lake didn't take much thought. Alex could drive the winding road in her sleep. She passed fields lined with corn rows ready for harvest and farm stands selling summer vegetables and field flowers. Wishing for sweet peas, she pulled off the pavement in front of a rickety, wooden shack. The structure was barely standing, but the farmer still managed to stack baskets piled with fruits and vegetables from his fields on the shelves. After a quick stop, with a paper bag stuffed with peas, she slid back behind the wheel. Popping the sweet seeds into her mouth, she made her way back onto the road, continuing the drive to the lake, catching glimpses of cows gathering under the shade of maple trees and chestnut-brown horses roaming fenced yards.

Such pretty country...miss it...comforting...familiar... feels like I never left.

The old bridge over the canal on the lake road didn't exist anymore. She wasn't sure if it just fell apart on its own, or if it was so dilapidated the township had it removed. There was no getting over the water that way, so she drove around the canal to a dirt road that led to the lake. Without traffic, the ride took only thirty minutes, so she pulled in earlier than expected.

It all looked the same. The long driveway to the Ricci camp was right next to her family's circular drive. Both houses were brown shingled with peaked roofs and screened porches. Alex pulled up to the stacked wood pile and got out of the car. She looked around for activity, but it was peaceful. The trees rustled in a soft breeze and the neighbor's houses were uncannily quiet. Just then, the crunch of the stone in the driveway signaled a visitor, and Phil's car pulled in. Parking along side his garage, he walked back around to meet her.

"Hey, Alex, let's head down to the lake front. There're

still a few chairs by the shore. I'll grab a few beers and be there in a minute."

"Sure, Phil. Meet you there."

At last together, Phil handed Alex a cold beer. Taking a long sip, Alex spoke first.

"So, what's the big secret, Phil? You dragged me all the way to the lake, so spill it."

"Alex, I have something. I don't know how to tell you."

"Are you ok? Are you sick?"

"No, I'm fine. It's just that I found something out. All this time, I know you believed my father had something to do with Jake's death."

Agonizing over his words, Phil paused.

"Well, he did. He didn't just have something to do with it. I'm so sorry, Alex. He was behind it. It was just this past week. I mean, I just discovered all of this last week."

It seemed like she was hearing voices from under water. When they were kids, they'd play a hearing game. She'd back float in the lake with her ears below the waterline while Phil talked, then she'd have to guess what he was saying. It was just like that. Alex could hear Phil's words, except they were drifting to her, muted and muffled, even though he was sitting right next to her.

I knew it...all along...Phil's father...that bastard...he killed my husband.

"My father's health was failing, and I knew his days were numbered. While he was in the hospital, I was trying to spend as much time with him as I could, going back and forth from the office every day. I'd sit with him, and when he'd wake up, I'd talk with him until he'd run out of energy and fall back asleep."

Phil slowly pushed himself out of the weathered Adirondack chair. For a few moments, he didn't make a sound. He stood staring out at the lake. Alex didn't move from her chair. She slumped into the hard planks. There was no comfort to find from the stiff slats or from Phil's confession.

Phil struggled to go on.

"Last week, he took a turn for the worse, and I think for the first time he realized he was nearing the end. I don't know if it was a guilty conscious or a death-bed confession. He was drifting in and out and called me closer to him. At first, I wasn't even sure he was coherent. I thought maybe he was just rambling, but then pieces of what he was saying started to make sense. In the end, I heard enough to realize that he did what he did to keep Jake quiet. Jake found out about a money scam my father was engaged in. Jake went ballistic and threatened to turn him in to the authorities. The rest is the ugly history you now live with. I'm so sorry, Alex. I have to live not only with the loss of my best friend, but also the guilt that my family caused his death."

Coming out of her daze, Alex's tears matched Phil's. They sat together for a long while without uttering a word.

What is there to say...we both loved Jake, and nothing, not even the truth of his death...nothing...will bring him back. I don't want Phil to carry any of the burden his father imposed on him...this is all too much.

"Phil, it's ok. Do you hear me? I don't hold you responsible for any of this. It's enough you've had the courage to tell me. I beg you to let this go. Feeling guilty won't bring Jake back, and you have nothing to feel guilty about."

Hearing Alex's compassionate words broke down Phil's last bit of reserve. With head in hands, he sobbed with gratitude for his Alex's forgiveness. Alex wrapped an arm around his shoulders, quietly crying with him until neither had any tears left.

Recovering, Phil took Alex in his arms and promised to make amends for his father's deeds.

"Alex, I know how much you miss Jake. I do, too, but I also miss seeing you. I'm thinking about moving south and getting the Miami office back up and running. I'd be near you and be able to spend some time with Chris. What do you think? Would you get sick of me?"

Surprised, but happy to have her friend back in her life, she gave him a bright Alex smile.

"That's wonderful, Phil, I'd love that, and I'm sure Chris would be very happy to have you nearby."

Phil's smile told all...he was delighted to hear her response. He reached over to give her a soft kiss on her cheek. Their bond reaffirmed, the two old friends sat by the lake watching the incoming waves break into white froth against the shore.

Part I
Miami

Chapter 1
The Wreath
Il tempo non si ferma
(Time doesn't stand still)

A year had passed since Jake was killed, and now the man Alex held responsible for Jake's death was also dead. Don Ricci, the man who had wrecked her life, and had caused her months of mourning, was dead.

Sheltered 1,400 miles away in her Miami home, she'd remained unemotional by the news of his death, until she attempted to send sympathy flowers.

It started with a phone call to the old neighborhood florist shop. Her family had been doing business with Campanos for fifty years. As expected, Marge, the shop owner, answered the phone, offering no condolences, only matter-of-factly asking whether Alex wanted to send a wreath crafted with white roses and red carnations or a heart simply composed of red roses.

She hadn't cried in the twenty-four hours since she'd

heard of his death, but now she was shaken. She could hardly speak. Her voice cracked, and she barely answered Marge as she considered her response.

No intention of leaving the security of my home to fly north to Seneca, New York just for his funeral. As far as this busybody is concerned, I'm simply a family friend sending condolences...not the girl relieved that the bastard is dead and gone.

Never shed a tear over Don Ricci...my tears are for Jake...

The repressed grief from the past year's events unexpectedly turned her stomach as bile backed up into her throat. Pushing herself off the cushion, she made a beeline for the bathroom sink to spit out the bitter juice. Phone still in hand, she rinsed her mouth and made her way back onto the wicker chaise with crippling pressure squeezing her chest.

My God, I'm sure I can feel my heart hurting.

With words trapped in deep breaths, she muttered, "Pull yourself together. You're just trying to order these damn flowers."

Alex crept from the chaise closer to the window.

Feeling compelled to send condolences...surely not out of respect for Ricci...out of respect for his son, Phillip.

The shopkeeper waited for a long moment, probably tapping her foot, then coldly inquired, "By the way, Alexandra, are you coming home for the funeral?"

Coming home? I haven't...considered...

Hearing the news the previous day hadn't really registered. She hated Ricci, but had been unresponsive to his death, until the agony of losing Jake had sharply resurfaced. The simple act of ordering sympathy flowers shook her to her core.

"I don't know," she blurted.

Embarrassed by the small-town gossip, Alex turned away from the window and slid back onto the soft lounge cushions.

"Well, you have plenty of time to get here," repri-manded Marge, "plenty of time until the funeral."

Alex's reply stuck in her throat and silent tears streamed down her cheeks. Exhausted, and cloaked with a blanket of sadness, she barely whispered, "A wreath."

She ended the call and quietly placed the phone back on the table hoping she could separate herself from the un-nerving question, "Are you coming home?"

Alexandra, Alex, as her family had nicknamed her since her tomboy days, remembered being told Ricci favored her...like a daughter.

What a joke...couldn't be farther from the truth. No one ever got close to him...no one ever really mattered to Don Ricci...Inseparable from his son, Phillip...my best buddy since childhood, not ever close to Ricci ...demanding, controlling...I still hate...people deferred to him...for no other reason...than he was powerful and connected...he never deserved the respect he received.

Ricci's most loyal ally, Alex's mother, Valentina, hadn't pressured Alex to fly home to attend the funeral. When Val-entina called the day before with the unfortunate news, she'd left the question hanging in the air. Valentina had her own his-tory with Ricci and enough of her own pain. She didn't need to hear Alex tell her why she didn't have to come home. Some-things were better left unsaid.

All these months, Alex wanted Don Ricci dead. She loathed him and craved vengeance for her husband's murder and the destruction of her life. Over the last year, she attempted to cast aspersions against him, but nothing ever stuck. She had no proof. At times enraged, she'd imagined killing him herself, but she knew that was just a fantasy.

Now, *what? He's dead...doesn't made me feel any better today than I did yesterday...my wealth...this home...all of it can not replace what I've lost. If wishes could come true...bring time to a screeching halt...turn the clock back a year...maybe I could change everything. Who am I kidding...wishful thinking...too late. Nothing is going to change the past.*

Alex sighed in defeat. "Ricci's death isn't bringing my Jake back."

Jake was dead and though a year had passed, the pain hadn't.

Lying motionless against the soft, chintz-covered cushions, Alex stared at the ceiling. She usually loved the feel of the smooth, glazed fabric, but today nothing felt right. Not moving from her bedroom since that late morning call, her thoughts tumbled from one to the next, always circling back to Ricci.

Dear lord...I can't focus on anything...except that bastard.

Agitated and chilled from the night air, she moved back toward the open window. Sunset long past, pale moon beams cast a faint light into the darkness of the empty sky. The heat of the day had come and gone, and the intense Florida sun had long since passed from the glory of an early evening sky to one of nothing but pitch blackness.

Drained and not able to stare into the heavens for one more second, she slammed the balcony's French door. Instead of closing, it banged against the door jamb and bounced back open. Reaching out to grab the doorknob, she froze as a flash of light streaked through the forbidding sky. Pausing, she watched the falling star's trail until its tail disappeared into the heavens. She mused, "Is that an omen or a sign of good fortune?" There was no way for her to know. The one thing she knew for sure was that everyone was waiting.

Chapter 2
The Abduction
Lussuria, amore e virtù
(Lust, love and virtue)

Sprinkled along the Gold Coast, Mediterranean Revival estates were seldom listed for sale, but once they entered the market, they were quickly purchased. Among the most beautiful, Alex's home, Villa D'Oro, stood out. Growing out of lush, tropical landscaping, this gem of a house sat perched on the edge of Biscayne Bay.

Each day, the stucco walls reflected the yellows and golds from the last glow of the sun's rays and held the heat at bay as they had for almost a century. Flanked by stone pillars, the driveway entrance stood regal with ornate, iron gates that opened smoothly with the push of a remote. The keystone drive ran straight from the road and then curved to the left, leaving the main house visible only from the waterside. Circled by a five-foot wall topped with coral stone dug from the nearby ocean, the estate sat privately away from prying eyes. The front path, lined with delicate peach impatiens, came to life when the tiny buds reached full bloom and filled the beds with soft, round mounds of color. Large terra-cotta pots, overflowing with white gardenia flowers, flanked the front gate, and the intoxicating perfume greeted all who approached the entrance. Hundreds of white and pink begonias twisted along the base of the stone wall, circling the property like swirled icing on a party cake. Just inside the brick courtyard, the bright shock of pink bougainvillea branches climbed and bent overhead, sprinkling the sky with mini, heart-shaped flowers. Sky blue petunias puffed and trailed down the sides of the Italian clay pots, marking the path along the loggia to the shady side of the house. Freshly planted each season, blossoms in mounded clusters and long, swirling rows bloomed from warm fall to humid Miami summers. Most days, the locals who lived along the bay stopped on their neighborhood strolls to admire the splendor of the blossoms and the natural artistry of the lush grounds.

The historic, land-marked home was built in 1929. The courtyard bricks were imported from Spain and the clay-roof tiles, salvaged from buildings in Cuba, were shipped on cargo boats to the old port of Miami. Natural coral stone, speckled with seashell remnants, was harvested in the nearby ocean and cut to create artful tiles that surrounded the pool deck. Beneath the broad-hanging eves, carved ornaments accented arched windows, each opening to the Florida sun. French-styled balcony doors brought the evening breezes into the grand bedrooms, making for a tropical oasis. The only markings to identify the address were the words *Villa D'Oro* scripted in old brass letters secured to the stone pillar at the estate's entrance.

A staff of three full-time employees lived close to the road in a series of small cottages. Tucked under spreading Ficus trees, the bungalows, with sloped roofs, arched doors and tilted chimneys, appeared to be drawn from a fanciful story book.

*

Carlo Manotti, one of the workers, had been living on the estate since his arrival in America from Salerno, Italy, in the 1970s. Similar to Alex's family's immigration in the 1920s, he pulled up his roots in Italy to come to America. The only difference was he'd left Italy out of necessity, not desire.

Carlo's, only brother, Franco, had a good life in Italy, so he stayed in his home country pursuing a career in real estate. Meanwhile, their baby sister, Sofia, spent her childhood dreaming of joining Carlo in the States. The three siblings stayed in touch with yearly visits and frequent phone calls. Carlo beamed when he connected with his family on those long-distance calls. "Hey, *fratello! Come stai? Tesora mio,* my sweet Sofia. Their loving kindred banter traveled across the miles as Carlos' hearty laugh echoed throughout the grounds of Villa D'Oro.

Cara, Carlo's wife, now a stunning beauty, became an orphan when she was eight-years-old. Her parents died in a canoe accident on a mountain lake during an outing near their home. Unlike most Italians, Cara had no extended family, so at their deaths, Cara found herself alone and a ward of the state.

Fortunately for Cara, her parents had volunteered for many years at the religious convent just outside of town. Her father helped the nuns with minor repairs, and her mother, an excellent baker, donated delicious cassata cakes for the sisterhood's holiday fairs.

Knowing her parents for many years, Mother Superior stepped in and requested guardianship when Cara became orphaned. Mother Superior was confidant there was no better place to put a parentless eight-year-old child than a cloistered abbey. Custody was an unusual request, especially coming from an elderly nun, however it took Cara off the state's books, so the petition was quickly granted.

A quiet girl, she grew to womanhood in the Catholic convent near the mountain ridge of her parents' fatal accident. All went well until, against all odds, at 17, Cara met Carlo.

In the early 1970s, quite cognizant of the financial difficulties of the times and wanting to fill the coffers, Mother Superior granted access to the nurseries from the surrounding towns to buy trees from the well-stocked and very overgrown convent lands.

Before emigrating from Italy to Miami, Carlo worked for a well-known botanical garden in the ancient section of Salerno. Assigned to locate saleable trees, he was surveying the abbey's grounds looking for strong specimens when he spied Cara hanging laundry just outside the convent garden.

Quietly making his way closer to the stunning vision, Carlo's deep voice startled Cara.

"I can't imagine a young girl as beautiful as you is living at this convent preparing to become a nun."

"No, no, I'm not. I mean...," Cara stammered a reply. "Yes, I live here, but I'm not a nun. I mean, I don't want to... I will not be one."

Carlo smiled, but before he could answer, she was gone.

Embarrassed by the conversation, Cara turned away and hurried to the washroom to finish her daily chores. For the rest of the day she tried to focus on her work, but it was to no avail.

Cara was comfortable living in the nunnery, but a desire to experience more from life had been building in her deepest core ever since she'd reached the unforgettable turning point of sixteen-years-old. She felt nothing but gratitude towards the nuns and a sense of peace hidden away in the nunnery, but that was all. There was no excitement, no challenge, no future except what had clearly been planned for her. That night, thinking about the young man in the garden, she twisted around in her sheets until she kicked them off and lay naked, staring at the ceiling.

Desiring this ripe beauty, over the next few months Carlo found excuses to return to the convent. Whenever he'd pass Cara in the yard, he sensed he was stirring a new excitement in her. Already a man of the world, he longed to hold her in his arms to be the first to caress her young, inviting body.

Cara lived a life of freedom as long as she stayed on the grounds within the convent's domain. The nuns felt secure in the guarded environment of their sanctuary and didn't feel the need to oversee her movements while she was close by.

As the months passed, she'd become more and more aware of Carlo and the effect he was having on her. Meeting Carlo made everything in Cara's world change, but she had no one to confide in. Like most days now, her imagination swirled around nothing but Carlo.

So, their timing was fated.

It was a hot, steamy afternoon. Humidity hung in the air like a damp blanket over the convent and the surrounding land. Cara had been working just beyond the rise in the abbey garden.

While tending to her chores, wisps of blue-black hair fell over her forehead, turning into feathery curls that embraced her face. Beads of sweat spotted her brow and the soft down of her facial hair moistened above her lip. Her full, shapely breasts moved with her slow breathing as the dampness of the day made her soft, white blouse stick to her skin.

Brushing her hand across her forehead, she slowly turned. Frozen, she gazed across the drying laundry at Carlo.

A red flush rose to her cheeks.

Carlo enjoyed watching her startled reaction as a frantic look flashed across her face. He didn't speak as he studied her with his dark eyes. They were not strangers in their dreams.

"Cara, let me help you. It's so hot in the sun. It's high noon now. Come with me to the stream. The cool water will refresh you."

With a whisper, Cara sighed, "Carlo, I don't think I should talk with you. It feels so wrong. I mean, it feels right."

Growing up in her cloistered world, she'd had no reason to know the facts of life, but even as she stood frozen in her confusion, she recognized there was something she yearned to learn.

"Sometimes what feels good can seem wrong, my dear. You know there's something here." Carlo motioned his hand back and forth between them. "There's no denying it."

He nodded his head in the stream's direction.

Cara hesitated, then followed. Once he was sure they were out of view from prying eyes, he moved to her side, brushing the damp hair off the back of her neck. Carlo sensed her confusion, but he didn't stop.

Carefully taking Cara's hand in his, he led her farther away from the nunnery. Guiding her to a grove of chestnut trees, they sat leaning against a sturdy trunk tucked away from the sun's beating rays. Carlo moved to the stream's edge. Taking his white handkerchief from his back pocket, he soaked it in the cool, moving water. Without hesitation, he pressed the cool cloth against her forehead.

Cara heeded Carlo's moves and waited.

I'm floating...where is he taking me...no...turning...back.

Carlo moved the cloth, slowly circling the back of her neck. Her nipples were now pushing through the pure white fabric of her damp blouse. Slowly, he took her silken hair in his firm hand and tilted her mouth to his. His lips pressed her lips softly as his tongue teased them to part. With a slight tug, he pulled the lace strings to undo her blouse. Unable to control his desire, he caressed her breasts with his lips and quickly slid his hand up her skirt. Fingers probing, he cradled her body and laid her back onto the soft grass.

Cara's arms circled Carlo's muscular back as she pulled him to her.

Excited by her arousal, he teased her with tiny kisses scattered up and down her neck. Feeling her quivering response and not able to resist a moment longer, he quickly slid her panties down her slender legs. With her breasts free to the air, and her skirt scrunched around her waist, he entered her and together they spun in pleasure.

Minutes passed and silence surrounded the two lovers. A cool breeze brushed across Cara's exposed nipples, and the afternoon sun warmed Carlo's bare chest. Wrapped in each other's arms, they laid silently watching the clouds drift across the afternoon sky.

In the weeks that followed, Cara yearned for Carlo. Whenever she could sneak away, she'd meet him without the embarrassment she knew she should feel. Captivated by his charms, she'd make love with him in the grass by the stream where it all began. Now a young woman in love, she'd lie naked, cuddled in his powerful arms, with nothing but the heavens above.

What had started as a conquest for Carlo slowly turned into something very different, as he struggled with his feelings for Cara.

Her soft voice fills my dreams...my first thought in the

*morning...my last in the evening...I'm falling in love...with
Cara.*

Love or not, he knew the nuns would never sanction
their relationship. He couldn't imagine a way to approach the
Reverend Mother for permission without creating a predicament in which he'd lose Cara forever. He considered every angle, but continued to come up with nothing that would guaran-
tee their future together.

Unlike Carlo, Cara wasn't dreaming of their future.
Most mornings, she was feeling ill, so time was dragging on for
her. One moment she was fine, but the next she could barely
pull herself out of bed to tend to her chores. Realizing her time
of the month had not come and fearing discovery, she said
nothing to the nuns.

Clearly unaware of Cara and Carlo's lovemaking, the
Reverend Mother assumed Cara had an obscure malady, so
she put her to bed while praying she'd get well.

The following week, Carlo came by the convent again
with the pretense of needing to buy more trees, but he couldn't
find Cara by the laundry or by the stream, so he casually inquired about the young ward.

"Mother Superior, I see your garden hasn't been
weeded and there are so many vegetables that have ripened.
What has become of the young girl who tended them?"

Suspecting nothing, the venerable nun sadly responded,
"She has taken to bed with vomiting sickness. The poor child
is beside herself, and we can't figure out the cause."

The nuns had done their best to protect their charge
from the world, but their best hadn't been good enough.

Carlo was not naïve and surmised the cause of Cara's
illness.

In that moment, he recognized the necessity of acting

immediately.

I can't live without Cara...I must steal away with her and my unborn child.

As he stood in front of the Mother Superior, his plan quickly materialized.

He reached down to the white daisies growing by his side and snapped a bunch in his sturdy hand.

"May I take these, Mother, to the young lady? If she is up and about, I would like to see a smile on her face. Maybe if she sees something from the earth, she might want to help herself grow healthy again and return to God's work in the sun."

The gesture seemed so kind and so innocent. The nun nodded and motioned Carlo toward the cloister's ancient courtyard.

He followed the winding path in and out of fenced hedges until he finally came upon Cara resting on a wooden bench next to a bubbling fountain. Her beauty had faded and despair had replaced the glow he so loved.

"Cara, the nun tells me you are not well. Are you still feeling ill?"

Accepting the flowers, Cara brought them to her nose. Without raising her eyes, she murmured, "I don't know Carlo. I mean, yes. I'm so confused. Everything is upside down. I mean, I'm pretty sure why I'm feeling sick." Moving off the bench closer to the fountain, Cara ran a delicate finger through the dancing water. "I didn't know at first, but I know now. I have no one here to talk to, and I'm making myself mad."

Furtively looking around the secluded garden, Carlo took her hand.

"I love you, Cara. I will never leave you. Please listen to me. I have a plan to take you away from here, so we can have a life together. You must find a way early tomorrow morning to meet me at the stream as you have before. If the nuns see you walking in that direction, they won't be alarmed. They know you like to stroll by the water and will suspect nothing. If you leave by early morning, the chances of someone spying you will be slim. I'll be at the water's edge waiting for you."

Feeling a sense of relief, but controlling the rising panic in her chest, Cara whispered, "Meet you to go where, Carlo?"

As he wiped away a tear droplet from her cheek, he whispered, "Cara, I love you. There is no time to explain. Please trust me. Please be at the river at daybreak. I must go."

As he turned to leave, their eyes locked in confirmation, and his genuine smile gave Cara the first hope she'd had in weeks.

Passing an unsettled night in the only home she'd known since childhood, Cara tossed and turned, her worries keeping her awake.

Exhausted from a sleepless night, she rose in the dark before the break-of-day and quickly filled an old satchel with her favorite sweater, a knitted wrap and some odds and ends of clothing. Not wanting to leave without taking something of her past, she scanned her modest room for memories and finally settled on three sentimental objects—her mother's locket, an old, tan cap her father used to wear, and a wooden cross the nuns had given her when she first arrived at the convent. Stuffing them in the pouch, she turned and took one last look at the life she was leaving, and then she quietly closed the door.

Without dawn's light, she cautiously made her way. Tiptoeing across the cold, stone floors down the deserted hallways of the ancient nunnery and finally through the empty kitchen, she silently slid out the back door. She'd hardly taken a breath since she left her bed from worry that the echo of her steps would wake one of the cranky nuns who hardly slept through the night. However, as the door latched behind her, she felt the cool morning air embrace her face. With the realization that the abbey still hung in sleep silence, she drew in a deep breath of relief. Following the twisted stone path to the stream, she mouthed a prayer for strength and guidance as she gingerly made her way through the dew-covered gardens.

Carlo, a man of his word, was waiting.

Cara whispered in the darkness, "My prayers are answered. Thank God you're here, Carlo. I didn't sleep all night, worrying you wouldn't be waiting for me."

"My night was also heavy with worry. I thought you might not come."

He took her in his arms and whispered, "I love you, Cara Mia, and I already love our child. I will always be by your side. Come, we must go now before we are discovered."

Hand in hand, Carlo led Cara down to the water's edge away from the nunnery, and the life she knew. He'd made a plan, and he was going to make sure it succeeded.

Hiding Cara in his tiny apartment until they could leave the country, Carlo focused on nothing but Cara and their future life together. He busied himself finalizing their departure while making certain a nosy neighbor did not notice her presence. Needing assistance, he shared his predicament with his brother, Franco. Franco had connections, so he contacted his associates for help, not only with orchestrating their getaway, but also with planning a clandestine marriage.

Cara had time on her hands, so the weeks became a blur. She never questioned her decision to escape the convent, and once they were married she resolved she'd done the right thing, but she still spent every day frightened the nuns would find her and pull her back. Hiding away suspended in the momentum of the long hours, she prayed Carlo knew what he was doing.

Days and weeks passed until finally, one damp October morning, Carlo woke her with a sweet kiss.

"It's time, my darling. We must go."

Cara let out a sigh of relief. "I've had faith in your ability to plan our departure, but truthfully I've been a nervous wreck. I'm thankful the wait is over."

Slipping quietly out of town with the early light, they made their way to the boat dock in Naples.

Their fates had aligned. Three months pregnant with their son, Carl, Cara landed in America with her new husband, Carlo Manotti. With Carlo's steadfast commitment to his new family, he found not only gardening work, but lodgings, and they quickly settled into a new life in Miami working and living on the estate at Villa D'Oro.

Chapter 3
Going Home
Amor di Madre, Amore Senza
(A mother's love has no limits)

Still immobile from the day's events and the conversation with the florist, Alex curled up on the lounge long past her
usual bedtime. She felt a breeze blow in through her second-
floor terrace door along with the intermittent sounds of Chris's
video games. Playing in the bedroom down the hall, the zing
and zap from the game's audio vibrated into the evening air
from his room to hers.

Looks like we're both restless...Chris can't sleep either.

She knew she would eventually heal from Jake's loss, but
wasn't sure how much it had affected her young son. He wasn't
sharing much, even though she tried to encourage him to talk.

*I can't bear the thought that Chris is in emotional
pain...This has been an overwhelmingly sad loss for him. He's
too young to understand death, but he clearly understands his
father is gone. He doesn't say much, but I can see his confusion
and feel his sadness.*

Alex remembered how much she and Jake had longed

for a child. They'd tried to get pregnant for several years and had been terribly sad to think they'd never be parents. They tried the usual medical paths, but the news was always a defeating, "no luck this time." But, as chance would have it, one sweet tropical night in August, either lady luck or the hand of God was with them. Christopher was born that following May to a joyful and grateful couple.

Life was so good...special times...rocking our little treasure...singing him to sleep...those sweet songs my Nonna Andrea sang to me...Jake's beaming smile lighting up the house...cradling his little guy.

Chris' lovable ways charmed and captivated. Fearless climber...staircase banister happily turned into personal slide... the sweetest child...

Life was so good...until it all disappeared...it had gone hopelessly wrong.

Desperate for answers, she called to the vast heavens. "What does my future hold? Will my life ever be filled with love again? I never imagined I could miss someone as much as I miss Jake."

Her anguished thoughts, interrupted by the pulsating sounds of Chris's games, Alex snapped back to the matter at hand. Her mind wasn't at ease knowing she had a funeral waiting.

A soft knock on the door interrupted Alex's musings. Mrs. Hermes quietly entered the bedroom with a tea tray. Treating Alex as if she was her own daughter, in her Jamaican lilt, she pleaded with Alex.

"Mrs., you must drink up some hot tea and taste these sweets I made fresh this morning. How can you refuse a slice of my coconut cake? Bless up, my dear. I worry about you."

Alex welcomed some coddling after the day she'd just

gone through. News of Ricci's death had turned her emotions upside down amplifying her sadness and her anger.

"You're the best, Mrs. Hermes. I'm grateful you brought the tea tray. Thank you so much."

Still dressed in white jeans and an oversized t-shirt, feeling the chill of the night, she tucked her bare feet under her legs. She was glad for the hot tea and the tea light Mrs. Hermes had set up on the end table. Staying warm, the tea took the chill off and brought a slight blush of heat to her cheeks.

How much longer can I gaze into this night sky...so tired...my energy...fading like the faint lights of the isolated fishing boats in the distance.

As the evening stars quickly filled the black sky, Alex realized what she needed to do. With the strength of Mrs. Hermes's tea, she carefully reached for the phone to call the airlines.

Decision reached, Alex made her way to Chris' room to tell him she had to go to New York and to ask if he would like to go with her.

I have no intention of taking him to the funeral, but he'll have a great time with the family...having Chris along... makes me laugh...he's a breath of fresh air.

"Chris, I'm so sorry I've been out of it today. I'm not sure if you heard the talk in the house, but there's been a death in Seneca. Mr. Ricci passed away, and I must go to the funeral. Would you like to come and spend some time with Nanna and your favorite cousin? I know Anthony would love to see you?"

"Wow, Mom! I didn't know we had a trip planned to Nanna's house. My cousin! This will be a blast. Oh, I'm sorry for your friend, Mom."

Sorry for him...I guess I am...really didn't like that man. I'm sorry for us. She thinks I don't know...things aren't ok...miss my dad. It hurts...so mad... lonely...angry...help-less...pushing it all down inside. Everything is different. Trying my best...strong...got to be strong. Play my games...go to school. Can Mom do this...can I do this...got to keep go-ing...got to be strong.

Alex couldn't hug him fast enough.

Even in his excitement, he's sweet enough to offer his regrets...truly is the light of my life. I only hope I've kept enough of the ugliness away from him...protect him... truly not sure if I've succeeded.

"Thank you, honey. That's very kind of you to say. Do you think you could pack your own bag? It's really late, and I'd rather not wake Mrs. Hermes."

"Sure, Mom. That'll be easy enough. Can I bring my Nintendo?"

"As long as you actually pack clothes, of course. We're leaving early, so how about I help you, and then we can both get some rest."

With very little sleep, Alex woke fighting a tight grip of anxiety pulling at her chest. Going over her last-minute checklist, she sat at her vanity, looking directly at her reflection in the mirror.

I guess I'm pretty in an exotic sort of way...

The golden beauty of her radiant skin, luxurious hair and proud walk made it impossible for her not to be noticed.

"So what," she cried, as she pushed back from her dress-ing table. "I might as well look ordinary for all the happiness my looks have brought me."

I'm being silly...not the truth. My life's been crushed and looking beautiful or ordinary has nothing to do with it...every-thing to do with the man who is lying cold in that Seneca funeral parlor...the man I'm going to fly 1,400 miles to see.

Mrs. Hermes knocked softly. The morning light shone through the white linen curtains, and the morning air was sweet and warm, but Alex was uneasy with trepidation about the days ahead.

"Carlo took your bags downstairs, my dear. He has the car waiting to drive you to the airport. I understand from Mr. Christopher, he's joining you. He's been jumping around for the last hour. I could hardly get him to eat breakfast."

"Yes," Alex smiled, knowing how much he'd be missed. "You'll just have make do without him for a few days."

Chapter 4
The D'Amatos and the Riccis
A tavola con la famiglia, non si invecchia
(At the table with family, you don't get old

The flight to New York was uneventful and gave Alex time to reminisce about her youth. She'd grown up in Seneca, living her whole life in the township, until she left for college. After graduation, she'd never gone back there to live, but she had never lost her family ties. Her parents and her extended Italian family all lived in the valley, so she spent months visiting every year from long, Adirondack summers to cold, snowy Christmas holidays.

A carefree childhood...that's what I remember the most, especially the endless summers spent at our family house on the lake. So funny...I remember school letting out in June and thinking it would be a year before September rolled around for the next grade to start...the mind of a child...saw no time.

The Riccis also had a summer home, the next house over. Phillip Ricci was only one year ahead of Alex in school, and Alex was a tomboy, so by the time they were pre-teens, they'd bonded like siblings and could talk to each other without the need to say a word. Oh, the trouble they got into!

Confined to her seat on the plane, Alex floated back through time to her childhood memories with Phil at the lake.

"Listen, Phillip," Alex whispered, with her hand cupping her mouth. "Why don't we make a plan. The Manna kids spray painted the tires on our bikes, so we must get them back!"

The neighborhood kids, who lived down the lakeshore, were sort of our friends. Sometimes we all got along, and then other times we were rivals. This summer, I wasn't sure what started the trouble, but I was in for the long haul.

"Retaliation? Yes! What do you have in mind this time, Alex?"

Phillip always showed interested in my mischievous ideas. He usually went along with my pranks and many times was the one to cover for me when we got into trouble. I knew he didn't mind. He loved being around me, especially playing the hero protecting me from the world.

"Well, I think we should plan a war. We'll hook up all the hoses around the house and push them under the crawl space, so no one sees them, and then we can fill water balloons and store them to use as..."

Before I could finish my sentence, Mr. Ricci came around to the lakefront where we were sitting under our favorite oak tree. The tree was the source of plenty of fun. We climbed its branches and many an afternoon sat up almost to its peak, looking high across the lake. It was exhilarating for us to swing from its limbs that jutted out over the shore to fly high and crash into the cool water.

Some days the lake water was fresher than others. To-day, the algae had rolled in and there were dead fish tangled in seaweed stinking up the air. One of our jobs was to rake the seaweed out of the shoreline and get rid of the dead fish, not a favorite of our assigned chores.

"Hey, kids, how's it going today? You two look like you're up to no good."

Mr. Ricci was not my favorite person. Not that he did anything in particular that I could put my finger on. It was just that there was something about him, like an aura or something that had always bothered me. His aftershave turned my stom-ach...maybe Jade East...I'd get a whiff...close my eyes to stop the feeling of falling, like plunging helplessly into a deep, dark well.

Witnessing my darkened face, Phillip quickly replied, "Nothing, Dad. We're just hanging out trying to figure out what we should do today."

I watched Phillip's features go from relaxed to tense.

He can't say anything...Phil never answers his father back...too scared...doesn't like his father much either.

"Well, if you need something to do, that algae is thick today and there must be at least a school of dead fish snarled up. Nothing wrong with cleaning that up, is there?"

"Sure, Dad," Phillip piped up. "We will be happy to get rid of this smell."

I didn't let my face show my true feelings...It's bad enough Phil is looking like his father...his voice is sounding more like his father's voice every day...surely don't need two Mr. Riccis in my life.

"That's great, son. I'm off to work for the day. I'll be sure to check on your progress when I get home for dinner tonight."

As Mr. Ricci turned to leave, I gave Phillip a look that could kill. Now, we were stuck for the next few hours cleaning the lake front. There wasn't a school of fish, but enough of a mess to keep us busy.

"You're a total jerk, Phillip! Why did you say yes? You could have kept your mouth shut. Now, we're committed to this nasty job. I should let you do all by yourself."

"What did you want me to do? You know my dad. Even if I didn't respond, he would have expected the clean up anyway."

"Fine, let's get going, because we have a war to plan."

The Ricci and the D'Amato families had been *paisanos* for years, both families coming from the Campania region of southern Italy.

Many of the Italians living in Seneca, and the surrounding towns in upstate New York, had ancestors who came over on boats to Ellis Island a generation ago. In the early 1900s, southern Italy was a poor land, so there was an exodus of Italians who came to America to find a better life. Some were escaping lives they never spoke about, while others just wanted to start fresh and experience the new world. Along with the comfort of the familiar, many left their parents behind and endured rough journeys across the ocean.

It wasn't a coincidence that once a few families arrived from a village, others would follow and settle nearby, recreating their lives as best they could. Most came with nothing more than a trunk filled with all their worldly possessions. It was difficult to be an immigrant in this land of gold, so their traditions, their foods, and their family values provided comfort as they banded together in the older neighborhoods

Alexandra D'Amato and Phillip Ricci's ancestors were no different. Their grandparents made their way across the ocean in the early 1900s. Once established, they made sure their children learned to speak English. Most importantly, they expected their children to study in school and to stay close to the family. They understood leaving the "old country" and starting again wouldn't be easy, but they weren't going to throw away their chance at starting over. Hard work was what they knew, and it was instilled in the next generation, so they survived and thrived.

Alex's maternal grandparents also followed the pattern of so many other immigrants coming to America to start a new life. Placing their love for each other and their families above all else, they were the Daleos, Andrea Fiorano and Giuseppe Daleo, Nonna and Papa to Alex.

Nonna never said much about the journey across the Atlantic, other than she'd been a young girl of 18 leaving home for the first time on a very long and difficult voyage. Her Giu had saved money and was blessed with a gift from his friend, Tino, so he had enough to purchase cabin passage and to settle in the new world. Nonna always touched her heart when she spoke about her Giu. She loved Alex's grandfather with all her heart and felt their seven children were a gift from God, Andrea's mother, Valentina, "Tina" named after Giu's old friend, Tino, being the sixth born.

Cooking together on Sunday mornings was a beloved routine, so everyone in the family arranged their schedules to make sure there was time to meet at Nonna's house. Even with a first-floor modern kitchen, Nonna cooked in the basement kitchen where the gas stove warmed the room and the savory aroma of her red sauce filled the air. Nonna Andrea was still a strong woman who cherished those Sundays with her home full of love and laughter. She especially adored spending time with her granddaughter, Alex, who was a younger image of herself. Both very strong willed, Andrea saw herself in Alex and was always available for a morning coffee chat or an afternoon talk. She was a steadfast example for Alex of the importance of being her own woman, and she encouraged Alex to have faith in her own decisions and to follow her dreams.

Wrapping her arms around her granddaughter, she whispered her words like a prayer, "God has blessed me and given me much more than enough."

"Your grandfather, bless his soul, always knew people. A man in Naples, I recall his name was Lorenzo, put him together with a man in Seneca, so we were not lost when we got off the boat. We made our way here and found a place to live and to work, and we made a life…"

No sooner would Nonna be in the midst of one of her stories, when a relative would come from behind and squeeze the air out of her. She'd feign being disturbed, but everyone knew she loved it.

She'd be starting the dough for the raviolis or rolling the pork and beef for meatballs when one or more of Alex's aunts, uncles, or cousins would storm into the kitchen. Everyone knew Nonna would be making Sunday dinner and getting a quick, fried meatball before it hit the sauce or stealing a chunk of bread to dunk was a weekly treat. Andrea was as quick to slap a hand reaching into her frying pan as she was to turn and embrace a face with love. Before she knew it, her old Formica chrome-trimmed kitchen table would be full of family, all talking at once, sharing the news of the week.

By the time Alex was in middle school, Andrea's beautiful curls, still thick, had faded to grey, but for as long as Alex could remember, they were pulled up and secured with an old, ebony comb. Her shapely arms had rounded out with her bust and her belly, and her hands were crepey from years of work, but her bright smile and the light in her eyes never faded.

As in many families, Andrea had a favorite sibling. Hers was her brother, Luca. Parts of Andrea and Luca's story was vague or just unspoken. Alex was never sure about some of their history, but understood not to ask. She did know that after Nonna came to the States, Luca missed her terribly. He was a party boy until she left for America. Then, things changed.

When Andrea left Italy, Luca discovered that his sister had guts. She had done what he hadn't had the backbone to do. Disobeying their father, she'd left her town and her family for the new world. Luca not only admired her courage, but also leaned on it to give him the strength he needed to do the same.

Despite the natural beauty of his hometown, he truly didn't want to spend his life stuck in the hill town of his birth where everything stifled him. He saw the same people every day, went to the same church and walked the same streets. Mostly, the way of life was old to him. Luca knew early on that staying in Sicignano working for his father was too suffocating. He knew the routine would kill him if he stayed. He also wished for the freedom to be his own person and to live his own life. He needed change. The weekends he'd spent in Naples cavorting with his friend, Gino, hadn't been only to sew wild oats. They'd also been an escape.

When his sister left, he realized he needed more from life than fast nights in Naples. Returning to his hometown and his childhood sweetheart, Ana, he persuaded her to travel with him to America. So, with his younger sister as an example, and a hopeful heart and a new wife, Luca also found his way to a new beginning.

The unspoken bond between Andrea and Luca and their history made them inseparable. Reminiscing over their childhood memories of growing up together in Italy, they each provided a little bit of home for the other. Luca and Andrea's children grew up best friends. The American family grew, and the generations moved forward together.

Luca, only a few years older than Andrea, showed up in her kitchen on Sunday mornings. The years hadn't always treated him well, but he'd accepted his fate. Losing his wife after many wonderful years of marriage, he felt fortunate that one or more of his four children always accompanied him. His black wavy hair was gone, and he was left with a shiny, bald head and stooped shoulders, but Luca was a grateful man. He'd followed his dream to come to America and had built a life he'd only imagined and hoped for. So, it was more than enough to be sitting in his sister's kitchen surrounded by their families with a Sunday dinner cooking on the old gas stove.

The warmth of close family, like the warmth of her grandmother's kitchen, was the world Alex knew. Connected and blended, they stuck together and built bonds that couldn't be broken.

The enemy...sneaky...feigning friendship...only to strike...no words for this betrayal. How could this ugliness happen? We were like family...never liked ...devious...lurking Ricci, but murder...especially my husband. So much ruined because of our dearest family friend.

The seatbelt light flashed. The pilot's announcement, notifying they'd land soon, broke into Alex's thoughts.

Turning to Chris, she checked to make sure he was

buckled in tightly. Trying to shake out of her somber mood, she snapped her seat tray closed and buckled her seatbelt. More to herself than anyone else, she groaned under her breath. "Well, it's time to face them all. I have a funeral waiting."

Chapter 5
Beginnings
Buon seme dà buoni frutti
(A good beginning makes a good ending)

Driving east from the airport took 50 minutes. Alex had been landing in Syracuse for years, taking the New York State Thruway to her childhood home in Seneca. On most trips north, she'd anticipate the days ahead with excitement, knowing that family and good times were waiting. Keeping with her family's traditions, they'd gather around the kitchen table, feasting on the best homemade food made from family recipes brought from Italy several generations ago. Telling stories, they'd chide each other until the room filled with laughter.

But this time, it was terribly different. As much as she'd promised herself that it was time to move on, driving to go to Ricci's funeral brought her nothing but sadness and fueled her repressed anger. As she sped along the highway, she reminded herself, " I'm going only to make sure he is dead."

With Chris next to her, sound asleep in the passenger's seat, Alex turned on the local soft-rock radio station.

Rod Stewart crooning "Tonight's The Night" softly filled the silence in the car. The long, empty road rolled along in front of her.

My love for Jake and sadness for my loss triggered by an

old love song... Jake use to serenade me with the first few lines of this song...

As tears slid down her cheeks, Alex recalled her early years with Jake.

She'd met Jake Reed one weekend in Vermont when she was on winter break from college. Alex's friend, Beth, was an avid skier, so the two of them headed east. Once settled in the same quaint room at their favorite inn, they headed to the slopes.

Sitting shoulder to shoulder, as the gondola made its way to Killington Peak, all was fine, until Alex's binding released and her right ski dangled off the footrest into the air.

"Beth, my binding released. How am I going to ski out of this gondola on one left ski?"

"There's nothing I can do to help you. I can't bend over far enough to reach your ski. Just keep trying!"

Perspiring inside her heavy parka, she reached down to grab the clasp to pull her ski back up to sit on the footrest, to press her boot back into its binding. For a few minutes, it didn't look like she could connect her ski, but just as the gondola door slid open, it landed back on the foot bar and the boot snapped into place. Relieved she was skiing out on two feet instead of one, the girls slid out of the gondola. Not paying attention to the trail signs, they pushed through the white powder down a short, back slope through a row of trees. Coming out of the bend in the woods onto a long, open stretch of white, they nodded to each other to take the hill. The snow was perfect, and the weather was calm. But, within moments, they knew something wasn't right.

"What the heck! How did we get here, Beth?"

"I don't know, Alex, but this isn't good." Beth adjusted

her goggles as she tried to size up the obstacles ahead.

For years, Killington's mogul line was known for the steepest bumps. Intermediate skiers, without real experience, didn't belong on this mogul run, but the girls were at the top of a mountain with no way to go back. With no choice but to ski, they began the struggle down the hill. Beth and Alex didn't speak. Their energy was spent maneuvering the terrain.

As they approached the base of the mountain, their adventure got worse. A large banner reading *Finish* stretched across the slope. Stationed under the pennant, the men's ski team cheered them on. The girls were mortified. Crossing through the chopped powder at the base of the slope, the girls ignored the rowdy celebration and disappeared into the chalet away from the clapping and cheering.

Finally seated in a booth, Alex groaned, "I'm so embarrassed, Beth. Can you believe our luck? That will teach us to pay attention to the trail signs."

Laughing as they helped themselves to the complimentary cheese fondue, they agreed it was definitely not a hot chocolate day and ordered two large glasses of merlot.

"Excuse me, but didn't I just see you finish the mogul run?"

Alex turned to see a handsome young man, the corners of his eyes crinkling and smiling along with the rest of his chiseled face.

"Yes, you did. We crossed the finish line. If you came here to tease us, just get it over with."

Realizing his smooth tactic hadn't worked as planned, he put up his hand in an apologetic signal.

"No, not at all. I just wanted to say that was really something. I mean, getting down that hill without falling. I'm Jake. I work here on weekends. I go to Boston College."

Jake was rambling on as he stared into Alex's beautiful brown eyes

His face was slowly turning red. Alex smiled, realizing he was flustered. Strangely, she felt an instant familiarity, as if she'd known him from some place before. Tilting her head up toward him, she smiled in response.

"So, why don't you join us, Jake from Boston?"

That was thirteen years ago. They'd fallen in love, graduated from college, gotten married and had this wonderful son who was sitting next to Alex as she drove along the New York State Thruway. Jake should have been driving them along the highway to Mr. Ricci's funeral, but Jake was dead thanks to Mr. Ricci. Alex couldn't prove it, but she knew he'd had her husband killed.

That fortuitous day in February in Vermont had changed her life. Nothing could compare to what started that day in the ski chalet after the most ridiculous and embarrassing moment of her young life.

Jake became her everything as their lives blended together.

When they first met, Jake was in his last year in Boston College, before heading to a two-year MBA program at Harvard. After her graduation, already deeply in love with Jake, Alex moved to Cambridge to be with him.

Alex's best childhood buddy, Phillip Ricci, also became Jake's best friend. Alex worried that she wouldn't be able to keep her close ties with Phil, once her relationship with Jake grew, but to her pleasant surprise, there was no competition when they met, only camaraderie. Phil, also a business major, found a great deal in common with Jake beyond the fact that they both loved Alex, so the three of them became best buds, and all was terrific in their young world.

Months moved along quickly and at the end of the two years, Jake was ready to move into the financial world. His smarts, serious studying, and degrees opened all the doors he'd hoped for. Opportunities came in from all the top companies in the Northeast. It was just a matter of selecting the offer that fit their lives the best.

They planned to marry after Jake's graduation. School finished, with job offers pouring in and wedding bliss on the horizon, made that summer memorable. Wanting to be closer to home to plan their wedding with her mother's help, Alex suggested they move into the family's house on the lake for the summer. Their lease was up in Cambridge, and they weren't sure where in the Northeast they'd be living, since it all was going to depend on Jake's job selection.

Summer was perfect as one warm day rolled into the next. Mohawk Lake hadn't changed a bit since Alex was a girl. The dead fish still caught up in the lake algae along the shore, and the summer sunsets still blazed orange across the early night sky.

Jake fell in with her relatives as if he'd always been a family member. He wasn't Italian, but he also loved tradition and longed for the tight connections he found in Alex's extended brood. His family consisted of only of him and his younger brother, Matthew, so Alex's clan filled in what he was missing the most-aunts, uncles and cousins, all knowing each other's likes and dislikes and each in the other's business. At times, it was claustrophobic for Alex, but seeing the interactions through Jake's eyes made it all seem fresh again.

As always, an invitation to the lake house was open to one and all, so whenever Jake's brother, Matt, could get away from his job in Boston, Alex's family included him. Close as brothers could be, the two boys had gone into completely different fields. Unlike Jake, Matt's interest was in law enforcement and rather than following in his brother's footsteps, he went into the police force. As Jake excelled in school, Matt excelled on the force. Even though they didn't get to see as much of each other as they wished, they could always depend on each other knowing their loyalty was unwavering.

As they did when Alex was a kid, neighbors who lived along the lake, still gathered evenings on the lakefront, toasting marshmallows over open fires. Summer weekends rounded out with Phil, who was now working in his father's investment business. He'd become a regular, along with his father. Mr. Ricci would quietly join the festivities toward the end of the evening, not showing interest in anyone. Keeping his distance, he'd sit back in his Adirondack chair away from the group. Everyone showed their respect, but knowing his reputation, most kept their distance, except Valentina. Being neighbors for countless summers, they'd built a bond over the years. She'd think nothing of pulling up a chair next to him and chatting on for hours. Alex's stomach turned as she'd witnessed a touch of Ricci's arm or a whisper in her mother's ear. She'd never liked Ricci and didn't like him any better now that her mother looked like she did.

Before Alex met Jake, her dad, Salvatore D'Amato, died. He was a quiet man with a sweet smile and a hearty chuckle that filled her heart with warmth. Even though he was a man of few words, he somehow impacted the lives of everyone around him. Alex's heart ached for all the moments of her life with him that were now tucked away memories. She was saddened that Jake never met her dad; instead he met Ricci.

That summer, Ricci took an interest in Jake. Everyone knew Jake was getting offers from the best investment firms, and Ricci was no different. He'd call Jake over to sit with him on those nights at the lakefront showing interest in Jake's decisions. Having no history with Ricci, Jake welcomed the attention and accepted it as a compliment. This powerful and wealthy businessman taking an interest in him made him feel important. Jake was a born athlete and excelled at both summer and winter sports. So, being a golfer, it was an easy ask for Don to invite him to play at his exclusive club. Jake jumped at the chance, and their weekly meets began.

Alex didn't want to burst Jake's bubble, so she didn't say too much to him about Ricci. She tried to discourage him from getting too close to Ricci, but her concerns fell on deaf ears. She didn't know exactly what Ricci's investment business was all about, but after listening to rumors her whole life, she did know that Ricci had powerful, underworld connections, and that information made her nervous. He was too smooth. His wealth had given him polish, and he knew how to look and play the part, but he never fooled her.

By summer's end, just as Alex expected, Ricci offered Jake a job. Not just a job, but a chance of a lifetime, with a high salary. The only caveat was that Jake had to sign a nondisclosure agreement and a ten-year contract. It was a no-brainer for Jake. He liked feeling important around Ricci. He enjoyed that the man had treated him as a son. He looked forward to making so much money that he and his new wife-to-be would never wish for anything. He'd spent his whole life wanting to be somebody, and this was his chance.

With Alex's hectic wedding planning, she didn't have the energy or the focus to deal with Jake's decision.

Then, as much as Phil complained about his father's controlling ways, he encouraged Jake to join the company.

"Jake, what a team we'll make. With your smarts and my influence with the old man, before long we'll be running the show."

Phil was the final push Jake needed to accept the position. So, with a handshake from Ricci, Jake forged ahead and signed on the dotted line.

Chapter 6
Hellos & Goodbyes
Il dolce far niente
(It is sweet doing nothing)

Summer passed quickly, and in no time at all, it was Alex and Jake's wedding day. The gorgeous dress, the stunning flowers, the beautifully written vows and a night of dancing under the stars made the wedding the social event their guests would talk about for years.

Through Don Ricci's graciousness, his country club opened its doors for a glamorous August wedding reception, even though Alex and Jake's families were not members.

It amazes me that things get done when Ricci wants them done. There's always been something so eerily calm about him...makes me anxious. But, here I am at my wedding reception...holding my champagne glass up high...toasting him in thanks.

Though the newlyweds had been living together for the last few years, their familiarity didn't take away the excitement of traveling together on their Italian honeymoon. Arriving from JFK, their first stop was Venice's Marco Polo airport. A wooden taxi swept them away from the airport dock.

Speeding across the smooth water toward the ancient city...shades of cool blue...wind in my hair...ripples playing along the lagoon's surface. It's beauty mesmerizes me.

With spectacular views of the Grand Canal, their hotel dominated the Venetian lagoon. Each morning, Alex and Jake sat under cheery, yellow umbrellas on the hotel terrace sharing bites of sweet melon along with forkful of Italian prosciutto enjoying Venice's morning sun sparkling across the vast pool of water. Hotel patrons smiled hello as they passed the young lovers' table, and waiters fell over each other with winks and smiles in typical Italian style.

During leisurely days spent strolling through narrow alleys arm and arm, they embraced and laughed as they got lost in the twisting Venetian passageways. Caressing and kissing necks and lips, they'd wander home close to midnight, finding St. Mark's Square eerily empty and magical with low-hanging mists creating mystical halos around the lampposts that guided their way.

From Venice, they headed to Fiesole, just north of the spectacular city of Florence. They tucked themselves away in the former fiftieth-century monastery turned hotel nestled on a hilltop amid terraced gardens overlooking the ancient city. The lack of privacy during the summer at the lake had led to stolen, fleeting moments of passion. But now they had all the time in the world. Days in bed making love, not caring if they rolled over their breakfast bread crumbs, they barely made it from their sumptuous suite to their glorious garden overlooking the city and the Duomo in the distance.

Their mornings began as their days ended, making love. With the morning light, Jake woke running his fingers along the curve of her spine. Whispering her name, he nibbled the back of her neck. Sliding his hand down and around her tight buttocks, he squeezed and searched until he found her sweet spot. Alex's body, still warm from sleep, reacted to his touch. Already moaning with pleasure, she rolled over into his arms as she wrapped her legs around his. Finding each other's lips and bodies familiar and wanting, together they greeted the morning, blended as one.

Still tasting Jake, Alex lounged on the garden chair, gazing out at the sunlit world over Tuscany as she sipped her morning coffee.

I'm feeling more in love with Jake and more connected to my heritage than I ever could imagine...pulling at my heart, warm...a sense of belonging...never felt before.

Not wanting to leave without finally visiting southern Italy, the honeymooners spent a few splendid days in Positano, basking under soft, warm rays on the sunlit beaches and cruising in and out of the rock formations on the crystal blue waters. Surrounded by cascades of pink roses, they curled up naked in cashmere throws making love on their hotel terrace. Pleasured, they'd end the nights watching the lights of Positano twinkle up the hill behind the tiled church dome of Santa Maria Assunta. Layer after layer of homes stacked like wedding cakes sparkled in the night sky.

Rising early on their last day in the cliffside village, they headed south to Sicignano degli Alburni to walk the streets of the town Alex had heard so much about from her grandmother, Nonna Andrea. The town in the province of Salerno in the Campania region of Italy, held her family's roots, and Alex was hoping to feel a special connection there.

Perched on the highest hill in Sicignano was the finest bed and breakfast in the southern countryside. This stylish, boutique hotel, with first-class service, was owned by Franco

Manotti. The picturesque setting provided a beautiful last stop on Alex and Jake's honeymoon.

The next few days naturally blended one into the next. *I'm walking the same streets my grandparents and great grandparents walked so many years ago...carrying me...back in time.*

Because it was low season and the young lovers were on their honeymoon, Franco Manotti, made it his business to make them feel welcome. Also, his brother, Carlo, was an American citizen now working at an estate in Miami, so Franco felt a special connection to his American visitors. After a few drinks at the bar, they got to know a bit about each other. Upon learning that Jake was an up-and-coming businessman, Franco offered to take him on a tour of the grounds to show him the inner workings of his business.

Alex wanted to be alone to soak up the smells and sounds, so she willingly sent Jake off with Franco. With map in hand, she wandered down a long, perimeter road to reach the local cemetery. Cimitero di Sicignano degli Alburni sat secluded behind a wall built of stones, shaded by ancient chestnut trees. Each gravestone held a photo of the deceased imbedded in the marker. She meandered, turning corners, squeezing through narrow lanes, reading family names. *Fiore, Pepe, Sorrentino.*

At last, she found what she'd been searching for, an angel engraved in worn, grey granite, swept its wings over the name *Fiorano*, her mother's family. Such silence was to be expected, but this quiet was beautifully accented with birds chirping and the rustling of leaves in the bowed trees. Settling on a stone bench smooth from years of weathering, Alex relaxed, daydreaming.

Startled by shuffling footsteps, she looked up to glimpse a bent-over priest, draped in black robes hanging from his feeble shoulders, walking toward her. Realizing he'd surprised her, he stopped and put his hands together with a slight bow of his head.

"*Mi scusi. Mi dispiace. Non volevo spaventarti.*"

Understanding his sentiment, Alex quickly replied, "No, no, it's okay."

"Ah, Americana! So, you speak English. Let me try after all these years. I am the retired padre of this church."

Pointing up the hill to the stone church in the distance, he formed each English word carefully.

"May I ask your name?" he smiled as his eyes slowly followed to the gravestone behind Alex.

Rising to stand, Alex softly replied, "I'm Alexandra D'Amato. On my father's side, we are the D'Amatos and on my mother's, the Fioranos."

The old priest was stunned. Alexandra looked so much like Andrea, the girl he'd almost married, the girl who had left him at the altar on their wedding day. She had the same wild, wavy hair. Her eyes had the same amber fire that he remembered in eyes from so long ago. Standing in front of him was the image of the Andrea of his youth. He stood at almost a century old, staring into the eyes of the granddaughter of the girl who saved him. He grabbed for his chest and moved to sit on a stone bench by his side.

Concerned he'd taken ill, Alex took his arm and helped him to sit. He was speechless and sat quietly for a moment. She reached into her backpack and offered a fresh bottle of water.

"Please, Father, maybe some cool water will help you."

Nodding his head, his shaking hand gratefully took the bottle. After a slow sip, the color that had drained from his face gradually returned. Not knowing what had just passed through the priest's memory, Alex thought the warmth of the afternoon air had caused his lightheadedness.

"Thank goodness, Father. You're looking better. Is there anything I can do for you? Would you like me to walk you back up to the church?"

"If we walk slowly, I'd like that, my dear. Maybe on the way you can tell me about yourself."

Alex nodded as she took his arm and began telling him about her recent wedding. She told him about her parents, and about her grandmother, Andrea, and her life growing up as an Italian American. By the time they reached the side door of the church, the padre was out of breath.

"Alexandra, may I invite you into the church for a minute? There's something I'd like to show you."

Alex smiled and again took his arm as he leaned and put some of his weight on her. The interior of the church was cool, and the air was sweet with the pungent perfume of burnt incense. He moved toward an alcove to the side of the altar. A white marble life-size statue of Mary stood in the center of the curve.

"Alexandra, look at these stone plaques in the marble floor around the statue. These are plaques dedicated over the years by the parishioners to honor and remember those we loved and those who were important in our lives. Do you see this one?" The priest pointed to a worn, bronze plaque embedded in the white stone.

This can't be...my grandmother...What's her name doing....engraved on this plaque?

In Loving Memory
Andrea Fiorano
God Bless You and Keep You
Forever In Our Hearts

"Would you sit with me? I'd like to tell you a story."

As the old priest came to the end of his story, he reached out for Alex's hands to cup them in his.

"So, you see, my dear girl, I am the Marco of the tale Andrea never told. Your grandmother saved me. Those days were not like today. On our wedding day, she ran right through that door with my secret in her heart as she made her way to her true love, your grandfather, Giu. I don't know how I would have survived the shame if she told what she knew. After that fortunate day, I thanked God by serving him my whole life. Your grandmother was a true friend, and I've prayed for her all the days of my life."

Alex leaned forward and patted the old padre's feeble hands. Marco drifting back from his memories, raised his head as he felt her touch.

"Father, would you like to thank her yourself?"

"Myself? What do you mean?"

"She's alive. My Nonna Andrea is still with us."

"She's alive," Marco repeated, more to himself than to Alex.

"You aren't the only one who has been blessed with a long life. My nonna has always been a robust woman who held my family together all these years since my Papa, Gio, died. Her health failed recently, but she's very much still with us."

Reaching for her cell phone, Alex called Andrea. In just moments, she heard her grandmother's voice.

"Alexandra, are you all right? Why are you calling me on your honeymoon?" Like a typical Italian grandmother, Andrea's first thought was that something was wrong.

Alex quickly replied, "I'm fine, Nonna. We're fine. Everything is okay. But I have a surprise for you. I met an old friend of yours here in Sicignano. He's sitting right here with me in Saint Matthew's Church. He told me a story saying he wished he could have thanked you for saving his life when you were just a young woman living here."

Andrea reached for the back of her kitchen chair to steady herself. She felt a shiver as a cool breeze brushed across her neck. It all came flooding back, their friendship, the wedding, Marco's secret, her elopement with her Gio. All these years, she wanted to tell Marco how sorry she was. Coming back on the line, she finally spoke.

"I shouldn't be surprised, my dear Alex. There are no coincidences in this life. This was meant to be."

Hearing her grandmother's response, Alex turned the phone over to Father Marco.

The Marco mystery is finally solved. No wonder the name, Marco, was a whispered story my grandmother never told.

The old friends spoke for the first time in decades. Each talking at once, they reminisced and laughed as if no time had passed. Alex stepped aside to kneel at the alter to say a prayer of thanks knowing that finally Andrea and Marco had the chance to mend their friendship with forgiveness and love.

Franco returned with Jake that that afternoon. They'd become friends during their outing and were enjoying a good laugh in the hotel lobby bar. Patting Jake on the back when he saw Alex walk in from the sunlight, Franco beamed, "Well, my dear, my instincts were right. I knew I'd be crazy about you and this guy. How about drinks all around?"

Stunned by Father Marco's sad story and drained by the heat of the day, nothing appealed to Alex more than a cool glass of the local, white wine. As the three new friends sank into the cool leather of the bar banquette, Alex wanted to tell Jake and Franco about the tale she'd just heard, but knew she'd keep that secret tucked away as her grandmother had done all those years before.

At the end of the week, Franco wouldn't hear of them calling for a ride to get to the Naples' airport. With hugs and promises to stay in touch and to come back to visit, Alex and Jake waved from the car window as Franco's driver whisked them away from the town where so much had begun. Now, as they were about to begin their own journey back to America, little did they know the importance their new friendship with Franco Manotti would play in their lives and the ominous events to come.

Chapter 7
The Turning of the Screw
Le vecchie abitudini sono dure a morire
(Old habits die hard)

Refreshed from their honeymoon and eager to get on with their lives, Alex was busy looking for a house. Jake was fitting in at work and doing just fine. Making his way each morning to Ricci's investment firm working side by side with Phil, he was clearly happy with his decision to take the job.

The day had started with an invitation from Ricci asking Jake to stop in for a drink at the end of the workday. The request wasn't unusual, since Jake had had plenty end-of-the-day celebratory drinks with the boss before. He excelled at his work, and he knew that Ricci's opinion of him was high.

But, this wasn't going to be a celebration for Jake. Jake was astounded by what Ricci had to say. He was being exiled to Miami, exiled with pay, but still exiled.

"Listen, Jake. I've been planning on opening a satellite office in Miami, and it all came together much faster than I anticipated. I need a good man to oversee this new endeavor. You know, get it off the ground, and make sure it succeeds.

This is a step up for you, young man."

Jake may have been young, but he knew how things were run, and this made no sense. Still standing stunned, Jake ran the scenario through his *head.*

Burned so many bridges...no way I can walk... not a man I can defy...he's spun a web..

"Miami is a promotion, an opportunity of a lifetime."

Yeah, right. I'm caught.. Why didn't he tell me before I accepted this job? No way he didn't have this plan in motion months before he buttered me up...offered a salary just above the highest offer I received...did he know about my other offers? He sucked me in...knew the connection with Alex's family put his offer at the top of the list. All I've ever wanted was to be somebody...ignored Alex's take on this guy...I felt important around him...I'm an fool.

Ricci made an offer Jake didn't refuse the first time, and now he made a second offer Jake couldn't refuse. Jake was intimidated and found himself accepting the strong-armed offer as he shook Ricci's out-stretched hand.

Jake returned home that night confused and distraught over the unjustified situation he found himself in. He'd passed up amazing job offers only to be banished to Florida. Hearing the news, Alex was livid. She ranted and raved marching back and forth while Jake tried to calm her down. He agreed with her, but also knew he'd have to swallow his pride and take the move like a man.

"Alex, please listen. I'm so sorry I let my pride get in the way of trusting you. I knew you were suspicious of Ricci, but I let my desire to feel important with a successful scam artist supersede everything else. Now, I have no choice. Please give me time to appease Ricci by opening his new office. Once I feel comfortable, I'll try my best to get untangled from his web and use my smarts and connections and get us back to New York. I'll figure it out. In the meantime, Miami will have to be home."

Phillip was also surprised. He told Jake that he didn't have an inkling these plans were in the making. He promised Jake that he'd have a talk with his father and try to change his mind. Valentina was in shock. She didn't react any better to the news than Alex, but didn't want to upset Alex and Jake any more than they already were, so she suggested that the move to the Sunshine State might be a nice change to live the good life on the beaches of Miami.

Chapter 8
Villa D'Oro & The Butterfly
L'amore di un padre vive
(A father's love lives on)

As luck would have it, Alex and Jake were still in touch by phone with their Italian honeymoon friend, Franco Manotti. On a very fortuitous phone call, they shared Jake's move-to-Miami predicament.

Franco inquired, "Jake, have you decided which area of Miami you want to live? Are you at all interested in buying a house on Miami Beach?"

"Yes Franco, I've been searching for a house in Miami on the water. Luckily, my income won't be changing with the move, so I can afford a big purchase.

Listening on the speakerphone, Alex chimed in, "I'm tired of talking to real estate agents. This isn't an easy search."

Alex really wanted to add her distaste for Ricci to emphasize the move was being forced upon them, but Jake stopped her in mid-sentence, seeing no point in sharing their anxiety.

Clearly happy to help his young friends and his brother at the same time, Franco asked, "Do you remember I told you about my brother, Carlo, who oversees the gardens on an estate in Miami? The family he works for is selling the house, and he's concerned that he and his wife, Cara, will have to look for another job. Would you be interested in speaking with the sellers?"

Not having their hearts in the search, this was music to their ears.

Alex chimed in, "Yes, that would be great. Please tell us how to reach them."

The rest was quick history. To Franco's delight, his American friends bought the house through photos and phone conversations. Besides buying the estate, they also promised Franco that Carlo and Cara could keep their jobs and continue living on the grounds.

Once the sale was final, Alex and Jake packed up their lives in New York and were prepared to make the move to Miami. They couldn't predict how the future would play out, but they agreed they'd do their best to accept the change.

Carlo was looking forward to meeting the new home owners, as well as relieved that he and his wife would be keeping their jobs. Villa D'Oro was the only home they'd known since they'd arrived from Italy. They were comfortable with the life they'd made in America, and they were not looking forward to any more change. He was grateful, and wouldn't forget the Reed family's kindness.

Move-in day finally arrived. The black SUV crossed the gated entrance as Carlo pushed a wheelbarrow full of dead palm fronds toward the house. The new owners, Alex and Jake Reed were arriving, so Carlo made sure to leave the main gate open. He hoped their first meeting would go well. Trusting his brother's opinion, he was sure everything would all be fine. He could see Mrs. Reed looking at him from the passenger's side window as the car rolled to a stop. She was staring at him with a look of surprise, and Carlo wasn't sure what to make of it. As she walked slowly over to Carlo, he put the wheelbarrow down and stood to great her.

A look of confusion spread across Alex's face as she put her hand out to shake his.

"Hi, you must be Carlo, Franco's brother. I'm Alex Reed."

She turned to Jake who had moved from the car to her side.

"And, this is my husband, Jake. We can't thank you, and your brother, Franco, enough for letting us know that this house was going on the market. Without your inside infor-mation, I'm sure it would have sold before we had a chance to put in a bid. Also, buying sight unseen isn't an easy task, so your long-distance help was priceless."

Alex tried to hold back the feelings she'd kept quietly inside since her dad's death.

I can't believe my eyes. His light olive skin burnished from the sun and his crystal-clear hazel eyes...looking at me with all the kindness I knew from my father...like looking into a pool of comfort and warmth...need to take a deep breath.

"So pleased to meet you. I feel like I know you, since my brother has so often spoken about you.. I'd like to be the first to welcome both of you to your new home. May your years here be filled with love and happiness."

While Alex and Jake were settling into their new home, Jake was doing his best fitting into his role in the new office. It wasn't easy, because Ricci directed everything from New York, and made it clear that Jake's position of Chief Operating Office was in title only.

Though Alex had been upset when Ricci had banished them to Miami, it didn't take long for her to become accustomed to the sunshine, the beaches and the balmy nights. Moreover, Villa D'Oro was more than she had expected in so many ways. She loved the house and the grounds, and focused on a renovation to reflect their taste and to truly make the home their own.

Her days were filled overseeing workmen as hardwood floors were sanded and polished until they gleamed. Stucco walls got a fresh coat of soft, white paint that changed color depending on the angle of the daylight streaming through the French doors. She discovered she enjoyed gardening, so it quickly became her new hobby. She ordered gardening books, and was delighted to spend mornings in the charming garden solarium that bordered the yard. She occupied herself arranging bouquets from the colorful flower cuttings she snipped from her extensive garden.

Their reluctance to move to Miami slowly shifted to an acceptance to stay. Jake didn't enjoy his lack of authority at his job, but otherwise things were going well, so they set aside their desire to move back to New York and focused on building a life together at Villa d'Oro. Years sped by, and life moved along for both the Reeds and their estate workers.

Carlo's black, wavy hair had turned to grey, and his face was now lined with deep wrinkles, along with creases at the corners of his eyes, from years in the sun. His back was a bit bent over, but he was still as physically strong as ever from his years of outdoor labor.

Jake had also grown a few grey hairs, and his temples were now shaded salt and pepper, but he was looking more handsome and distinguished with each passing year. He'd joined the Miami Beach Golf Club finding it was a great venue to bring in business and to make new friends. Entertaining at Villa D'Oro became a frequent event, and he was loving the life he and Alex created in Miami.

Alex enjoyed being a prominent member of the local community. Villa D'Oro's heritage opened the doors for her involvement in state and local historic preservation. She hosted fund raisers and holiday fairs to benefit the preservation of the homes built in the early 1900s. Her decorating skills, honed from her extensive renovation of their home, admired by their friends and acquaintances, drew plenty of attention. In no time, she was appointed to the golf club's advisory board to help with the building's renovation.

However, the role she cherished the most came to her and Jake as a pleasant surprise. After years of hoping for a child, they were blessed with the birth of an adorable baby boy. After four years of living on the estate, the quiet hallways and perfectly designed rooms quickly shifted to a bustling site of adults rushing to appease a seven-pound infant. Christopher, nicknamed Chris, became the center of focus for, not only his parents, but also for the household staff.

Baby bottles and a high chairs appeared in the kitchen and dining room, play pens filled the library and the family room, and baby carriages for leisure and jogging materialized in the entrance hall. As Chris grew, so did his toys, his school supplies and his list of friends. Sneakers piled at the front door and dirty t-shirts from playing T-Ball at the local park, brought a twist on life that Alex and Jake had never anticipated, but truly loved. Happily becoming the center of everyone's attention, his effect on the house and the people in it, made them a family.

Carlo was forever grateful that he and Cara were able to keep their jobs and their home at Villa D'Oro. They were equally relieved and happy when the Reeds grew to be, not only a wonderful family to work for, but a family they respected and trusted.

The warm connection between Carlo and the Reeds got even stronger as time passed. Missing the childhood days with his son, Carl, who was now grown and living on his own, Carlo fell head over heels for little Chris.

Over time, Carlo became much more than the grounds keeper. Jake was busy with his work, so he began to defer to Carlo regarding the workings of the house. Carlo still spent many hours with Alex working on the gardens, but as his job description changed, and age not being so kind to his knees, he hired a young gardener to do the heavy work. Now Carlo oversaw the house maintenance, supply inventory, and any and all workmen on the grounds. He was happy to take on new tasks, especially for this family that he'd grown to love.

Standing in rain-soaked grass, Alex's work boots squished each time she took a step. It was already another Florida summer and each day the afternoon rains cooled down the humid, afternoon air. Carlo was positioning a new crepe myrtle tree, twisting it this way and that way, waiting for Alex's approval.

"Perfect, that's it, Carlo, it's perfect."

Reaching for the shovel, Alex heaped a mix of topsoil

into the hole to form a mound around the tree.

Believing there was now a solid bond with Alex that had been built over many years, he felt the time was as good as it ever was going to be, so Carlo broached the subject.

"Alex, how long has it been, twelve or thirteen years, since you moved into Villa D'Oro?"

"You know, Carlo, I think it has been that long."

I've wanted to ask you something, but haven't wanted to upset you or pry. Can I ask you a question, but please know I won't take offense if you don't want to answer ."

"Carlo, of course you may. What is it you want to know?" Alex stabbed her shovel into the wet ground.

Carlo wiped his soiled hands on the rag hanging from his jeans.

"Well, the first day we met in the driveway, the day you came to live here, you had a look on your face that I really can't describe. You looked sort of shocked when we met. I've always wondered why."

Alex hadn't forgotten their first meeting and how meeting Carlo had rattled her. Motioning to a spreading Ficus tree, they sat beneath its branches shielded from the sun.

"Carlo, please don't think I don't remember that day. Let me answer your question by telling you a story.

I grew up with the most wonderful father in the world. He was a quiet, decent man, honest and hardworking, who tried his best to do the right thing. He was devoted and considerate and treated me like a princess. So, when I was away at school..."

The afternoon sun was fading as the tears were now quietly spilling out onto Alex's cheeks.

"I called to tell him about a great guy, who happened to be Jake, that I'd met. I can still hear my father's voice in my head.

"I trust your judgement, Alexandra. If you say he's a great guy, then I can't wait to meet him.'

"That was the last time I spoke with him. That night, my father passed away in his sleep. I was devastated from the loss, and I miss him all the time. I see him in my dreams walking through a beautiful garden. There's something in that dream that tells me he's okay, and I need to be okay, too. So, to answer your question, the day I met you, I was startled, because you are a mirror image of my father.

Carlo reached over and took Alex's hands in his. "I'm so sorry I brought this up, Alex. I had no idea. I'm so sorry for your loss.

Suddenly, a brilliant-orange Monarch butterfly flew past Alex's shoulder as she felt the warmth of Carlo's hands holding hers.

Alex lifted her eyes to the fluttering butterfly as it skipped close to her cheek and hovered in place for a moment as if it was taking her in. Circling just above her head, it landed softly on her nose, then swooped away.

"Something tells me, Carlo, you're not the only one who is listening."

Carlo couldn't believe his eyes, but then again, he knew there was so much in life that didn't have an explanation. From that day forth, Carlo promised himself to always watch over Alex like she was his own daughter.

Chapter 9
Jake Reed
La resilienza è la virtù dei forti
(Resilience is the virtue of the strong)

Jake sat behind his fancy desk in his Miami office thinking back over his life. Growing up in an Irish family, without a father around, in Charlestown by the waterfront, wasn't easy for Joseph "Jake" Reed, but it helped make him a man.

Charlestown, the oldest neighborhood within the city, was on a peninsula across from downtown Boston. Most people living and working there, like Jake's family, came from Irish immigrants who came to America in the mid-1800s after the Irish Famine.

My mom, Kathleen, came from family of four. Thank goodness my brother, Matthew, and I grew up with our mom's relatives...they filled the holes left by having no family on my father, Pat's side.

As far as I can remember, until about six years old, things at home were okay. There wasn't a lot of money, but we had enough. Living on the top floor of a green, clapboard triple-decker house was an adventure for Matt and me.

The Murphys lived on the floor below. They had two daughters, twins, one-year older than me. I remember how I'd clam up around them from nerves. I thought they were the most beautiful girls I'd ever seen, and they knew it. Loving that I'd get totally flustered, they'd flirt with me every chance they got.

Robert Kelly and his wife, Mary Kelly, lived on the first level. They'd lived in the weathered, clapboard house for forty-five years, starting when they were first married on the top floor and gradually making their way to the coveted-first level. Tired from years of work and families moving in and out above them, didn't make them for the cheeriest neighbors. Old-man Kelly scolded us for running up and down the back staircase and threw fits all winter long when he'd find wet-boot tracks in his back hallway. My mom repeatedly told us not to antagonize the Kellys. Most of the time, we'd listen to her, but we were typical boys.

My father, Pat, worked on the docks not far from our house. He'd come home dirty and tired six nights a week, not much of a talker, he'd eat dinner and then sit in front of the TV. My memories of Sundays, up to about six years old, were okay. The family would go the waterfront with a picnic lunch that Mom would lay out on a grassy knoll nearby. Dad showed us how to fish, so we'd spend the afternoon bringing in as much striped bass as we could, stacking the slippery-skinned catch flipping and flopping in a bucket of water and ice. As a family, we'd eat and doze on and off on the blankets laid out on the grass and listen to Dad tell stories of his days at sea.

As I grew older, I'd try to hang on to those memories, but time faded them and left me with the empty Sundays when my father wasn't home. He'd leave the house on his day off and come home after dark with no explanation. Mom, getting ready for Monday morning and all the work that came with it, didn't seem to notice. At least, I never heard her say anything to Dad. Then, when I was around seven, my dad skipped coming home a few days at a time. He'd leave on Friday, and none of us would see him all weekend. Sunday fishing at the wharf stopped, and eventually, so did coming home at all. It wasn't long before he just stopped coming home.

I'd grown to six feet by the time I was fifteen and took a liking to the quietest twin, Emmy. Even though I was a year younger than Emmy, I towered over her. Tall and confident, I wasn't such a nervous wreck anymore. Emmy was still flirting with me, so being more self-assured, I'd meet her on the back-hall steps to talk and eventually we'd kiss.

The twins were turning sweet 16, so a party was planned for the back yard. The families in our house didn't have much to celebrate, so the party was a big deal. Even the Kellys offered to help. Old man Kelly strung lights around the back porch posts extending the line to the weathered, side garage. Mary Kelly baked a beautiful, white, three-layer cake with "Sweet Sixteen" scrolled on top in pink icing. My mom, known for her Shepherd's Pie, was happy to make a stack for the occasion. Matt and I gave Mr. Murphy a hand setting up the folding tables and chairs while Emmy and Ella dressed the tables with pink and white paper cloths. Matt loved music, so he offered to put a few tapes together and set up stereo speakers in the yard.

The night was a success. Emmy and Ella's high school friends danced the night away to Marvin Gaye and Tommy James, along with Sly and the Family Stone. When the Beatles "Something" track started to play, I vividly recall slipping my arm around Emmy's waist and moving with her to the grassy *dance floor.*

From that dance on, Emmy and I were an item. We'd grown up together, living in the same house, so everyone thought we were meant to be. Emmy looked ahead to our life, married with children, while I similarly thought this was the path my life was supposed to take.

Then, time happened to us. I branched out at college and met so many new people. My classes opened my mind to all the possibilities in the world. I'd gotten good grades in high school, but now I blossomed. Principles of economics, mergers and acquisitions, investment analysis, I excelled at all of it. In fact, I couldn't get enough of it. My professors, recognized my talent, and challenged me. In no time I showed some amazing abilities and was on track to live up to my new nickname, the Wall Street Whiz Kid.

All of that future frightened Emmy. She was a small-town girl with small-town dreams. I did everything I could to make her comfortable in my new world, but the more I tried, the more she pulled away. Finally, we stopped talking about marriage and how many kids we were going to have. My classes took up more and more of my time until eventually I stayed at the dorm most nights and weekends. I saw what my life could be, and I knew I couldn't let Emmy stop me from my dream. Seeing what that life had done to my father and my parent's marriage, I realized that path wasn't for me. So, by my third year, when it was clear that Emmy didn't want or just couldn't grow with me, we ended it. There were tears from both of us. We'd started as kids together, so our young memories would always hold a special place in each of our hearts, but it was time for us move on, and I didn't look back.

Killington wasn't just a weekend job for me. It was a whole new life of sports and friends and an extension of my new college life. I was in my last year at Boston University, since I'd transferred from Massachusetts community college to BU in my junior year. I continued to flourish in my studies, coming a long way from the impoverished, Irish kid growing up on Boston's poor side of town.

Then, a mogul run changed my life. Alex and I laughed about it for years. I fell madly in love with everything Alex. She was beautiful, worldly and well-educated. She came from a solid, Italian background, so much like my mother's Irish family. Both raised Catholics, our holiday celebrations mirrored each other's. Her large family gatherings were everything I loved and wished for when I was growing up.

I remember holding my diploma across my chest with Alex under my other arm posing for the last of my graduation photos. I couldn't believe I did it. My whole life was ahead of me. I had the degree and the girl. My MBA from Harvard was going to open all the doors I could ever imagine. I was first in my class with job offers already pouring in. It was just a matter of deciding with Alex. Me and Alex. That's how it had been since the day we met.

After graduating, I took time that summer at the lake to enjoy life. After so many years of school, I felt I deserved a break. Early mornings we'd ride bikes to the state park with a thermos of coffee and homemade cinnamon buns devouring breakfast with our feet covered in sand and wet from the ripples of the cool water. Warm, summer afternoons were spent water skiing and boating across the lake.

Both Alex's and Phil's families owned lake boats, so most weekends we'd wait for Phil to show up and we'd party together into the night. I loved everything about that summer. My friendship with Phil and my love for Alex grew and grew. So did my friendship with Mr. Ricci.

Back then, I couldn't believe my good luck. Phil's dad took a liking to me. I'd never had a mentor. In fact, I never had a father figure to look up to, since my father walked out on my family when I was a kid. There were professors who encouraged me, but no one of Mr. Ricci's stature had ever taken an interest in me. By the end of the summer, I was a regular on Mr. Ricci's golf game, and Mr. Ricci was a regular at Valentina's dinner table.

I knew Alex held her tongue around Ricci for her mother's sake, but she was pretty clear with me that she couldn't stand him. Then the wedding plans took over, so Alex was totally occupied with invitations and all the multitude of lists that just kept growing. Before I knew it, Mr. Ricci offered me a once-in a-life-time job at his firm. I'd oversee high net worth portfolios with numbers I'd never dreamt of. I'd be right there in the main headquarters with Phil.

I knew how Alex felt, but how could I let her feelings for Ricci stand in the way of such an opportunity? So, I waited until the last minute to broach the subject, and her reaction was exactly what I'd expected. But, in the end I lucked out, because she was knee deep in our wedding plans and just didn't have the energy to argue with me. Besides, Phil would be working with me, so what could go wrong?

Chapter 10
The Con
Il malfattore non manca mai di scuse
(The evildoer never lacks excuses)

Jake was relieved that the Miami transfer turned out better than they'd anticipated. Slowly but surely, Alex put her personal stamp on Villa D'Oro, truly making it their own. Friends and visiting family, along with their wonderful household staff, buzzing around the stately 1920s property, created a climate for their family to blossom.

Alex also found a new hobby in gardening and was delighted to spend mornings digging and planting in the yard. They were fortunate the lethal, yellowing disease that hit Miami's palms in the late 1970s hadn't destroyed the coconut palms on their grounds, so Carlo showed her how to harvest and enjoy fresh coconut meat, so she could save the milky liquid for Chris.

Work was going well for Jake. He'd made a success of Ricci Financials' southern office, yet he never could quite figure out why Ricci felt the need to open it. However, knowing there was no use dwelling on that mystery, he let it go.

Glenda Martinez, Jake's secretary, also turned out to be godsend. Jake hired Glenda through a college friend, who previously worked with Glenda. When a new job offer in California came up, knowing Jake was heading to Miami, his friend suggested he hire Glenda. She'd been a loyal employee, and he felt confident in his recommendation.

Glenda focused on her job, and she was loyal to Jake. He appreciated Glenda's years of experience, and he valued her opinion. In return, Glenda had Jake's back, which was invaluable to him, because the office was run by Ricci and his man, Sammy Leon, who Jake saw as a very shady character,

Ricci had given Jake the title of Chief Operating Officer, but it was in name only. Ricci's right-hand man, Leon, ran the show in Miami. Ricci assigned Leon to the Miami office and made sure he took care of his bidding.

Ricci hired everyone in the Miami office, mostly inexperienced brokers and young, pretty assistants who came and went. Against Jake's wishes, he also assigned one of his New York crew, a man named George, to be Jake's driver

Jake did his job and collected his pay check.

Still don't understand why Ricci exiled me to Florida...maybe he just wanted us out of the way with Valentina...wasting my time going through the motions in an office that runs without much input from me...no question this office is run by Ricci and his boy, Leon. None of this has ever made sense.

Nothing made sense, until it finally did.

First, there was Michael Foster. Barely 30, he'd been welcomed into the office as if he was a seasoned investor. His connection was his wealthy aunt. Foster brought in millions of his aunt's money, and that made him special in the eyes of Ricci and Leon. He never seemed to put in much office time, other than schmoozing on the phone all the while, like a slick car salesman in a local commercial, sitting back with his feet crossed on his desk. Foster's quick rise to success and lack of work ethic turned Jake's stomach. But there wasn't much he could say, since Foster was the office golden boy.

All investors at Ricci Financials received monthly portfolio reports. As part of a yearly inventory, Jake asked Glenda to compare yearly gains and losses, as well as to print out a list of the client's names along with their contact information. That's when Glenda discovered what had been going on all along.

Glenda noted Mike Foster's aunt's address was missing on the main contact file. That was strange, since his aunt should have gotten a monthly report generated directly from that department. Then, just by coincidence, as she was walking by on her way out the door for the night, Foster threw a stack of mail on his secretary's desk. As Foster continued out the door, one envelope slid off the pile, just as Glenda passed the desk. She subconsciously picked it up to toss it back on the pile, but the handwritten name and address caught her eye. Not wanting to be seen, she quickly moved the envelope between the folders she was carrying. Jake was already gone for the night, so Glenda stepped into his office to turn his light off, carefully slipping the envelope into her handbag.

The next morning, Jake walked through the office door with his usual smile and good morning greetings. Looking around and not seeing Glenda at her desk, he assumed she was in the office kitchen getting coffee. But when he turned to enter his office, she was standing in front of his desk, motioning him to close the door.

"Hey, Glenda. Good morning." Jake stopped in the

middle of his office, tilting his head to the side in a questioning gesture. "What's up? Is everything ok?"

Glenda was furtively looking back out the glass wall and fidgeting with an open envelope in her hand.

"Mr. Reed, I wasn't trying to be nosey. I mean I was organizing the contact information for the clients, and I noticed..." Glenda was stuttering, which was not like her.

"Please, Glenda. Slow down. Have a seat. What are you trying to say?"

"The contact information for Michael Foster's aunt was missing on the monthly printout, the ones that get system printed automatically. You know, his big money client."

Curious, but thinking this was a lot of fuss over a missing address, Jake encouraged her to go on.

"Well, on the way out last night, Foster dropped an envelope, and when I picked it up, I noticed the address was handwritten addressed to his aunt."

Jake, now totally confused, said, "And?"

"So, I opened it."

"You what?"

"I know I shouldn't have, but what I found inside was worth getting in trouble for."

Jake was not one to preach, but he was someone who followed the rules, so he started to reprimand Glenda.

"Do you realize..."

Before he could finish the sentence, Glenda blurted out, "It was a fake report."

"Fake report"?

"Please, lower your voice." Glenda pleaded.

"When I went through the portfolio balances last week, it seemed strange that his aunt's balance was low. I mean, we all remembered what a fuss was made when he brought in millions of dollars of his aunt's money. Then, just this Monday, I overheard Foster telling Mr. Leon he was 'reeling the old lady in for big numbers,' and Mr. Leon chuckled. At the time, I thought those words were odd, 'reeling the old lady in.' Anyway, when I was reviewing..."

Jake still wasn't following. "Glenda, what are you trying to say?"

Flustered, trying to get the story out, she continued. "He sent his aunt a bogus report. The money is not in the account here, but the report shows all of it, plus gains."

Stunned, Jake slowly sank into his leather chair.

"Are you telling me the envelope you opened had a monthly report with false information?"

"Yes, and here it is."

Glenda quickly turned over the envelope.

"I know I shouldn't have opened it. I don't know what made me..."

Jake put up his hand, "Glenda, it's okay. We're past that now. Have you said anything to anyone?"

"I haven't...absolutely not. I've told no one."

"Ok, say nothing. Just go on with business as usual. Let me get to the bottom of this."

Not wanting to overstep her bounds any more than she already had, but not being able to help herself, she whispered across the desk.

"Jake, please be careful."

Jake watched Glenda through the glass wall. Sitting at her desk, everything seemed normal, unless you knew Glenda as well as Jake did. She was twisting a strand of hair behind her right ear, a nervous habit he'd noticed from when she first came to work for him. Pondering the seriousness of the situation, he hoped she could keep her cool until he could figure out what to do.

One thing he knew with certainty, he wasn't going to tell Alex about this discovery until he was sure he could prove wrongdoing. He didn't want to get her involved or have her call Phil and tell him his father was hiring crooks. He decided he wasn't even going to mention it again to Glenda. He didn't want to put her in a precarious position. Whatever action he was going to take, had to be done on his own. He had no idea who he could trust in the office, so he was going it alone.

Jake needed time to compile proof, so he lied to Alex. Feigning an overload of work, he blamed Ricci for overwhelming him with a time-consuming project with a looming deadline.

It doesn't make me feel good to deceive Alex...like nothing more than to spend time with my family...need to be in the office after hours... no one here to observe me...need to search through Foster and Leon's files...late at night...office is dark and abandoned.

It took weeks of clandestine searching, but Jake slowly started to compile enough evidence to prove securities fraud, money laundering, and egregious accounting fraud. Ricci's dubious methodologies were aimed at artificially improving the firm's financial outlook by creating off-balance credit sheets. Numerous clients, along with Foster's aunt, received inflated earning reports while Ricci and his cronies pocketed millions with their shady deals.

Running through the evidence, Jake smiled.

They thought they had the perfect set up...a small, satellite office no one would pay much attention...putting me in charge...they got a squeaky-clean Harvard graduate...an oblivious front man. I was naïve...exactly what they planned on. They buried the Miami information so deep...would have taken a special investigation to uncover the fraud. No one...until now...no reason to investigate. Won't be long before I take them all down...to think a dropped piece of mail was the start of their ruin.

Jake muttered under his breath, "I knew Glenda was a good hire."

On a few of those late nights, he'd come across the office custodian.

Think his name is Charlie...feel badly for him... probably fighting addictions...overly friendly...like a lot of stoners...might have been smoking grass on the job. My mother's words, "For the grace of God, there walk I."'...that adage carries a lot of truth. If I hadn't stayed on the straight and narrow growing up on the wrong side of the tracks, I might be in this guy's shoes...will ask HR to look at this character...not getting into it until I'm finished with my investigation...get back to handling the cleaning guy soon enough.

Alex sensed something wasn't right, because Jake was having difficulty disconnecting from the office. He'd always been able to balance his work and home life, but not lately. He'd been staying late most nights and returning home preoccupied with his work-related responsibilities. She worried that the job with Don Ricci was getting to be all too much for him. How she wished he'd never taken the position with that bastard. But Jake eased her worries, convincing her it was a short-term setback, and things would be back to normal as soon as he got through the assigned project. He promised he'd be back to spending evenings at home with her and Chris before she knew it.

Jake hoped that would be true. It took weeks, but he'd finally gathered most of what he needed to go to the authorities. It was another late night, this one being a Friday night. How he hated staying at the office instead of going home, but it was almost over. Grabbing a Coke from the office refrigerator, he turned to see Glenda coming through the open door.

"Glenda, what are you doing here so late? It's ten o'clock."

"Sorry to startle you, Mr. Reed. I must be losing my mind. I bought a cake today on my lunch break from Rendez-vous Bakery around the corner from the office. It's for my granddaughter's birthday tomorrow. Can you believe I left the cake here in the fridge? I'm leaving early in the morning to drive north to Vero Beach to celebrate with my daughter's family. With no time in the morning, I figured I'd better get it tonight. The one thing I had to remember to do, and I almost blew it."

"Don't worry, Glenda. You're not losing it. By the way, I haven't said anything to you about our discussion weeks ago. I needed to keep you out of it, but I want you to know if it wasn't for you finding Foster's letter, none of their crimes would have been uncovered."

"I was afraid to bring it up again. Please tell me you found enough to nail Foster."

Finally feeling secure enough from prying eyes and ears, Jake looked around the deserted office, and then smiled.

"Glenda, I can do more than just nail Foster. I have enough incriminating evidence to bring Sammy Leon down, as well as Ricci. Securities fraud, you name it. It's over. They're all going down."

Outside the kitchen door, standing silently against the

wall, Charlie, the night, custodian, froze.

What the hell did I just hear? This is unbelievable...he has no clue I'm here...how lucky can I get? I can use this info...get in good with the big guys...keep this job forever. They'll owe me...man oh man.

Slowly, sliding away, Charlie slipped down the hall and out of site into the office laundry. He'd keep busy in there until they left the building. They'd never know he'd overheard their conversation. He just scored his one-way ticket to a secure future.

Chapter 11
The Accident in Miami
Tradimento il peccato più grande
(Betrayal, the greatest sin)

Jake finally had what he needed to nail Ricci and his cronies, but he was wisely laying low until he finalized his report to the SEC. His plan was to file his accusations once he got back from Valentina's birthday celebration in New York.

However, Ricci unexpectedly dumped a project in Jake's lap telling him he was sorry he'd miss the birthday party, but the project was urgent and time sensitive and needed to be completed ASAP.

Confused by the last-minute assignment, but needing to remain cautious until he was ready to expose Ricci's scam, Jake didn't protest. It was the end of August, the last chance for the family to get together before Chris started school for the fall season. He wasn't happy he'd miss the birthday celebration or time with his family, so he promised Alex he'd get the job finished and join them in New York later in the week.

After sundown, the house gradually fell silent. Mrs. Hermes, age getting to her knees, said an early good night and slowly made her way to her cottage. Carlo waited for Cara to clean the kitchen while he sat at the counter working on the crossword puzzle he'd started earlier that morning

Jake never wanted a chauffeur, but Ricci had been adamant about having his "man in charge" of the Miami office serviced by a full-time driver. So, George took Jake back and forth to the office and to all his business meetings. He navigated all the airport runs, and especially took care of Ricci when he was in town.

He'd dropped Alex and Chris at the airport, sending them on their way to New York, and should have returned to the house until the end of his shift, except he was unexpectedly called away at the last minute with a family emergency. He wasn't going to be around for the rest of the night, but that was fine with Jake. Everyone knew he preferred to drive himself, so it was a given that he'd be okay using his own car wherever he needed to go.

Cara was almost finished setting the table for the next morning's breakfast, and she was ready to wrap up for the day. Content to be by his wife's side, Carlo collected his paper and turned off the kitchen lights. Holding her hand, they walked outside into the misty, night air toward their cottage by the gate. Just before they turned along the bend in the path, Carlo caught a glimpse of Jake in the second-floor library window and heard his raised voice.

Kissing Cara sweetly on the cheek, Carlo turned toward the main house.

"Cara, I just realized I forgot to check all the doors along the back of the house tonight. Go on in, and I'll be back in a minute."

"Are you sure, *mi amore*? I thought you checked earlier."

"I must be getting old. I may have, but I'll feel better if I make sure. I'll just be a few minutes."

Carlo made his way back to the main house knowing he'd already checked the doors. The closer he got to the house, the more concerned he became. Jake had closed the French doors, so his words were muffled from the outside, but Carlo could still hear Jake's raised voice. Once Carlo reentered the house, it was clear that Jake was having an argument with someone on the phone. Not one to eavesdrop, but also very protective of his adopted family, Carlo stopped in the foyer when he heard Jake shout.

"I can hardly hear you. Speak up. How dare you, Ricci? My wife and child? You son-of-a-bitch. You stay away from my family. I have proof, and I'm going to use it. What? Speak up. It's too bad I slipped somehow, or you'd never know what hit you. Sure, you know nothing about this. Tell that to the judge."

Then, Carlo heard nothing.

Again, Jake roared, "You can't hold that over my head."

Carlo couldn't hear Jake for a moment, then he heard Jake yelling again.

"I don't care. I'll take my medicine. I had nothing to do with your scheme. You're not pinning this on me."

Jake slammed the library door and stomped down the stairs. Carlo worried about what was going on, but not wanting to get caught listening, slipped out the door making it down the front steps to the driveway. Seconds later, Jake threw open the front door.

Surprised to see Carlo standing by his car, Jake questioned, "Carlo, I thought you called it a night a while ago?"

"I was walking the grounds and checking the doors. George is off tonight. Are you heading out? Let me drive you."

Knowing something bad was happening, he didn't want Jake going off on his own. Carlo rushed to say, "I've been eyeing your new BMW and wouldn't mind getting a chance to drive it."

Flustered and still fuming, Jake nodded a yes toward the car.

"Okay, Carlo. I just need to get something at the office. Pull up the back way into the garage and wait for me."

Jake didn't say a word on the 20 minute drive to the office. Traffic was light and the BMW quietly sped west on 395 toward downtown. The Miami skyline sparkled in the night sky as the lights reflected in the dark, blue waters of Biscayne Bay. A short curve through downtown brought them over the Brickell bridge and with a quick right they entered the underground parking lot that serviced the Ricci building.

Doing as he was told, Carlo let Jake out, pulled the car into a vacant spot, and turned off the ignition. A quick call to Cara, telling her he had driven Jake to the office, silenced her concerns.

Carlo put his head back on the soft leather.

Tired from a long day, he slouched down in the seat trying to get a minute of shut eye. Dozing off, Carlo was startled awake when a metal door slammed. He'd pulled the car into an unlit spot, so he was hidden in the shadows, but the building's exit door was still very visible to him. The security light from the garage roof illuminated the door, shining on one of Ricci's goons who was walking out of the building.

Carlo attempted to tie the pieces together.

This makes no sense...it's 10 o'clock...no one is supposed to be in the office...this guy has no real business here...only shows up in town with Ricci... stays by his side like glue. Ricci isn't in Miami...what's this guy doing here?

Carlo pulled himself lower in the seat, so he wouldn't be seen. Ricci's guy nervously looked right, and then left before turning the other way. He got into a black Mercedes and sped out of the garage.

Carlo waited a moment, but his gut was telling him something was terribly wrong. He quickly ticked the boxes.

Ricci stopped Jake from going to New York with Alex and Chris with a last-minute project. George, the driver...Ricci's man...mysteriously called away. If George isn't around...common knowledge...Jake drives himself. The call Jake just had on the phone with Ricci...must have been...to provoke Jake. Jake said...proof of something...supposed to only be in the office a few minutes...that's what he said...been at least thirty minutes.

Carlo jerked up in his seat.

Jake's being set up.

Impatiently waiting for the elevator and still fuming from the phone call, Jake mulled over Ricci's denials and threats in disbelief that he'd gotten himself in this mess. He knew the only way out was to use the proof he'd been collecting to put Ricci away. Jake couldn't imagine how Ricci found out about his covert investigation, but obviously he'd slipped up, and Ricci found out he was collecting information about the scam going on in the Miami office.

All those years of school and hard work to get to the top of my class, so I'd have a chance at a better life than the one I grew up with, only to get sucked into the world of Don Ricci. How naive have I been? Very, it seems. I had so many great job offers...accepted Ricci's proposition...that summer everything seemed to gel with Ricci being so close to Alex's family and Phil being my best friend. Then there was Ricci himself.

He groomed me from the start with the nightly talks around the campfire and the golf invites. He was scheming all along. The big surprise move to Miami, that was all in the design. Ricci needed a front, AKA the Miami office, to move his money and what better person than the super bright and very trusting me. Having a squeaky, clean newbie with a Harvard degree run the show while the real show was going on unnoticed was a perfect setup.

The penthouse elevator door opened onto the hushed foyer of one of the most stunning offices in Miami. African Mahogany doors marked the entrances to the four corner offices. Floor to ceiling glass circumvented all four sides, so the panoramic views spanned all of Miami south to Key Biscayne, north to the lights of downtown, and east to the ocean and Miami Beach.

I know I might have to pay a price for letting this scheme go on under my watch. I also know Ricci will try to incriminate me, since I'm the supposed head of this office. I'll just have to prove my innocence. Knowing what I know now...no choice...everything in my power to stop Ricci.

Rushing down the hall, he turned the brass knob on the mahogany door to his office. It was dark, except for the glow of the digital wall safe. Without flipping on a light, he beelined for the safe. His fingers were sweating as he pressed in the combo. The heavy door clicked opened.

Thank God...smart enough to set up this safe without Ricci being involved...never gave him the code. Here they are...the flash drives...everything I need to end this nightmare.

From his left side, Jake sensed a movement.

What the hell...turn toward the sound sharp-slamming-against the side of my head...agonizing...moaning...everything going white...humming...buzzing loud in my ears. I'm falling...Alex...Chris...faces...flashing.

Vito was glad he didn't have to wait too long for Jake to show up. Everything was going as planned.

Good...he went down fast...ha...didn't know what hit him...easy pickins'...not finished yet...gotta make it look like an accident. Ricci...paying me big money...saving himself...gotta get this job done right.

Vito went into action like only he knew how to do. He stuffed the flash drives into a leather satchel. With gloved fingers, he closed the safe and then dragged the unconscious Jake into the executive kitchen. A beautiful wall filled with restaurant-style gas stoves-just what Vito needed. He had it carefully planned out.

It will only take a minute for the entire kitchen to be gonesville...loud, but nearby offices are closed...streets are empty...gonna take a while for the fire to be noticed...by the time anyone gets here...this punk kid will be history.

Vito smirked as he muttered, "I'm gonna get another feather in my cap with the big guy."

Vito finished the job and exited the building through the garage just minutes before the planned explosion was to take out the employee kitchen and the unconscious Jake.

Charlie, the night custodian, knew he'd better not screw up this new job with Ricci Financials. Three months, he'd held down a job for three months. He'd made a few contacts with a couple of street people, but no one really knew him. He actually knew no one in town. He'd been drifting across the country for years and almost forgot where home was. A few OxyContins here and there, and he was getting through the day. Working a night cleaning job was a breeze. No one knew if he was a little stoned, and there was never anyone in the office to hassle him.

And now he'd hit the jackpot. Once he cornered Sammy Leon and told him what he'd overheard that night in the kitchen, he was golden. Charlie's smirk was spreading from ear to ear exposing his almost toothless front teeth.

I had my little talk with Leon...for sure...we're on good terms now...for real. That's right...going to get more money out of this little scheme...going to get lots of money. Imagine me...a steady job...no one breaking my balls and money in my pocket...these big shots owe me now...life is good for Charlie boy.

Tonight, I got a really good perk...the night off with pay. They'd started sanding the penthouse office floors...Leon said it made no sense to clean when there would be more sawdust, so leave early and take a few days off with pay. The floors are perfect, but what do I care if these rich jerks want to sand perfectly good floors. I'll score a few pills from my street buds and have a grand-old time for a few days with full pay...it's only a matter of time before Leon and his cronies pay me some big money for giving them the poop on Reed's big plan.

But, of course...messed this up, too...got stoned...before I even left the building...all the way home...forgot my apartment key...in the employee kitchen. Can't call it an apartment...two hundred foot dump in a broken down container by the river...still has a damn lock...don't have the damn key...standing at my shit-hole apartment with no key. No idea...who the landlord is...couldn't reach him anyway...late at night. This is what I get for raiding the office refrigerator...typical... loser...no money for dinner...key is on the counter.

"Shit. Shit. Shit."

Dragging his tired ass back to the office, he climbed up the back stairs. They told him to go home early, and he didn't want the boss to think he was up to no good coming back.

Maybe they'll think I'm trying to rob something. Crap. I'll just sneak in and get my keys... no one will ever know.

Fearing discovery, Charlie took the back staircase up to the top floor and sneaked into the kitchen surprised that the overhead lights were on. "Shit, did I leave the lights on, too?"

The bright, ceiling lights illuminated the entire kitchen. Charlie's eyes cautiously followed blood streaks smeared across the white floor tiles until they stopped at a body. Sprawled out on the cold floor Jake laid bleeding from the side of his head.

Charlie panicked and tried to reach for his keys.

I've got to get out of here.

A blast of heat blew him across the room.

The old, charcoal barbecue...remember...when... I was a kid. Mom's creepy boyfriend...told me to look inside...then he'd open the top...let the fiery coals singe my eyebrows...that asshole...no...no.

There wasn't much more Charlie would ever remember.

Suspecting the worst, Carlo's instincts reached high alert as he heeded his gut.

Jake was in serious trouble.

Adrenaline surging through his veins, he bolted to the elevator panel stabbing the up button. Sweating as he frantically counted the floors, the door slid open to a hair-raising crackle shattering the eerie quiet of the office suite.

Suddenly the building shook.

Barreling down the hall, he pressed against fierce heat as an invisible wall pushed back slowing his speed. Peering through fractured glass, Carlo spied flames licking the corners of the office kitchen. Ripping his shirt over his head and wrapping it around his nose and mouth, he barreled through the open door. "Oh no, Jake, no Jake."

Chapter 12
The Party at The Lake
Mangia bene, ridi, ama molto
(Eat well, laugh, love a lot)

Alex hesitated. *Hmmm...whew...party time...all these people.*

Sidelines a little longer before I step into this throng. Sky on fire...setting sun's rays-timeless like this lake. Everyone here...except Jake. My mother...radiant in her silk caftan... floating guest to guest...kissing cheeks in welcome. Warmth. Sweet Uncle Luca. Looks like he buffed his smooth, hairless scalp for tonight's festivities. It's shining under the flickering string lights strung tree to tree...Twinkle lights...Italy...maybe November...chilly. I think eight. Old village. Light strings. Must be why I love sparkling lights. Crazy how I remember that trip.

Nonna Andrea made it, thank God. Imagine Nonna and Father Marco. Umm. Uncle Luca right by her side. Lucky me...my roots all in one place. Kiss her in a minute. What's that song?..."Oh, what a night"...that's right. It should be a great night. Mom 65 tonight-as beautiful as ever. I don't feel great-whew-an effort to get in the party mood. Funny, lonely in a crowd...a void without Jake...stuck in Miami.

Oh, there's the culprit, Ricci. Look at him head to head with Phil and Sammy Leon. Don't they know this isn't a business meeting? What's with the furtive glances my way? I should glare right back at Leon, but it's not worth the effort. He's such a jerk. Old man Ricci better not come near me tonight. I could puke from his aftershave.

Oh, crap. Christopher and Anthony are going to knock over a table. I told my mother these boys should have stayed home with a sitter. So much for dressing them up. Too bad they can't act like their sweet cousins...so pretty in their party dresses whispering secrets down by the lake.

"Oh, hi. Yes, it's a beautiful party, isn't it. Enjoy!"

No idea who that is...maybe business? So funny. Aunt Maddy is knitting...in the midst of this party...needles clicking away. Uncle-ha...don't give him the mic...dapper, loud. Now...they all want the mike...Toasts...Laughs...Deserve this joy. Something just doesn't feel right tonight. Umm. Pink Veuve.

"Thank you, yes, so good to see you. So happy you made it to my mother's 65th!"

A few of these bubblies...just might put me in a party mood. Wish my Dad was here. I'll call Jake later...he'll want to hear all about this bash...here goes.

Long night...too much bubbly...my feet hurt...should have worn flats...wanted to look pretty. Thank goodness for Phil...saved me from his father's dance request. Eighteen aunts and uncles...stories to tell. What a family...cousins...so many...how lucky. Great 65th birthday. Too tired...must say goodnight...dear lord...that will take forever...the Italian 'good night'. Nonna Andrea...such sweet hugs. Mmm smells so pretty...like mom...soft cheek.

"Love you, Nonna. I'll stop and see you tomorrow."

A chance to talk with her without all this frenzy. Feels chilly all of a sudden...shoulders cold. Ricci coming...step away. Where's my wrap? Wish Jake was here...wonder if he's still in the office...missed the best party. Too late now...call him in the morning. Sky so black over the lake...where did the stars go? Uncle... reaching for the mic...so many toasts...so much to say...I am these people...all so proud...their stories...

Part II
Italy

Chapter 13
The Fioranos
Buon seme dà buoni frutti
(A good tree makes good fruit)

Alex's Italian family came from proud stock. Following their dreams, they'd persevered. With fortitude and resilience they'd crossed the ocean, took a chance and stepped into their futures.

In the early 1900s in a small village near Salerno, Italy, her great-grandfather, Vincenzo Fiorano, met her great-grand-mother, Maria Triane, when they were just children. They'd grown together into adulthood with the ease of always having the other by their side. Their youngest child and only daughter, Andrea, was an extraordinary girl with soft-radiant brown eyes and creamy skin burnished by the sun. The village beauty, she wore her silky, brown hair swept up and secured with her prized possession, a large ebony comb. Everyone knew her to be the perfect daughter.

Sicignano, a village of cheese and winemakers perched at the top of a hill, overlooked the most beautiful valley Andrea had ever seen. She loved her life growing up in the only home she'd ever known, but for as long as she could remember, she sensed a yearning deep inside for something more, or at least something different. She really wasn't sure what she felt, but she had an inkling her future wasn't going to be with her comfortable family in her picturesque town.

Andrea woke with a smile each morning, cheerfully ready to help her mother with the daily chores. Her deep-throated laugh could be heard, more often than not, drifting through the open kitchen window down the hill to her father's vineyard.

The beans were already boiling on the wood-burning stove and whiffs of the aromatic, roasting coffee floated through the air. Tiptoeing across the wet tiles still damp from her mother's morning ritual, she quietly planted a sweet kiss on her mother's soft cheek, "*Buongiorno,* Mamma."

Feigning annoyance, Maria shooed her daughter away. "Again, you surprise me, *mia figlia!*"

Moving about the kitchen, they busied themselves mixing flour and water into balls of dough for the family's bread and nightly pasta. Mother and daughter prepared the meals and made the house a home. One sang while the other hummed, and at times, they'd burst into lovely Italian melody. Maria loved her mornings with her daughter, and Andrea returned the love.

Before daybreak each morning, Vincenzo made his way down the hill to his vineyard, where his family had been making wine for more than one hundred years. Vincenzo believed a good day's work was the way to a healthy life, so he started his days very early. At Terrebella Wines he worked sunup to sunset alongside his three brothers and three sons. He took pride in his good family name and the fruits that came from their hard work.

When the kitchen chores were complete and the breakfast ready, Andrea walked the winding path to the vineyard to call her father and brothers to breakfast. Craving Maria's homemade bread and strong coffee frothed in foam, together they'd climb the hill under the first rays of the sun, enjoying the sounds of their wakening village.

Like most mornings, the warmth of daybreak's glow welcomed early risers as weather-worn shutters were unfolded to greet the dawn's light. Meddling women chattered back and forth, leaning out open windows with the first gossip of the day. Sweeping their stoops, they rambled on about the impossibility of living with their hard-headed men, the sadness of a neighbor's latest illness, or the rumors of an ongoing affair in the nearby village. Every day held a different story. The little children, already underfoot, prompted the first scolding of the day. Raised voices calling out. "Buongiorno," only added to the beautiful frenzy in their hillside town.

This morning, Vincenzo was unusually quiet, and he waved his sons ahead. With a nod of his chin, they understood they should make their way to the house. He'd follow with Andrea. Terzo, the oldest son, passing by just a few inches from Andrea's shoulder, turned walking backwards, looked her in the face and shook his head while he raised his eyes in disgust. He'd been upset with his sister for days, and he knew what was coming from their father.

Once alone with Andrea, Vincenzo broached the subject that had been brewing in his heart.

"Well, my sweet one, I've been told that Giu Daleo has been seen talking to you again. I hope you are not encouraging him. You know he is much too worldly for you. He is not the fellow for you."

Giu's father, Ernesto, had bad history with the Fioranos. Ernesto originally worked for Vincenzo. When Vincenzo fired him, he disappeared and left his family behind. His ten-year-old son, Giu, seven years later at 17, did the same. No one ever heard about either Daleos' whereabouts, until Giu, who was now 20, returned. The word had gotten to Vincenzo that Andrea had been seen talking to Giu after school down by the church cemetery. The news made Vincenzo furious.

Running the facts through his mind, Vincenzo fumed, "Andrea, Giu was an angry boy. Who knows where he's been for the last three years? He is not meant for you, and your innocent meetings will come to no good."

"Oh, Papa, we only talk and besides, he is so handsome, and he tells me about places I've never seen. His stories take me far away and ..." Andrea's breathy voice came to a quick stop when she saw her father's face.

Vincenzo moved abruptly to the side of the dusty street, stopping just before their house. "Andrea, *stai tranquillo!*"

Worried for his daughter and remembering the ugly events of ten years before with Giu's father, Ernesto, Vincenzo barked.

"This is not the first time I've warned you. You must not talk with Giu. He is not a boy, Andrea. He is a man who has left our village and has had a life that you know nothing about. His stories will fill your head and keep you from being happy here with your family. Someday you will meet a young man and marry. Then, you will live near here and raise a wonderful family. This man will bring you nothing but trouble. I will not allow this!"

To Andrea's embarrassment, his voice had risen to a shout. Her family had never been part of the town gossip, and now her father's words were sure to be repeated house to house. In her seventeen years, she'd never heard him speak to anyone this way, let alone her. Startled by his anger, she gathered herself and ran from him with only her tear-filled words trailing behind.

"Oh, Papa, you don't understand."

Running up the hill away from her father, all she could think about was Giu. Andrea had a secret, and she was never going to share it. In fact, she never told anyone how she'd met Giu Daleo.

One day...walking along the river...I grew tired...I tucked myself away in my hide-a-way cave to rest. Ever since I was a little girl...unbeknownst to my family...I've been coming to my secret place just under the tree line. Most days, I'd watch the water move along the shore...imagining where the river led...what the world was like at the river's end. That day, not accustomed to anyone ever being near my inlet...a rustle in the brush startled me. I quietly wiggled my way back into my cove...but, I'd been seen. An attractive young stranger...appeared in front of the opening. He tilted his head and looked at me suspiciously.

"Excuse me, my dear. Do you always make it a habit of sitting by the river in a cave by yourself?" His eyes twinkled with jest as he bowed. "Please let me be a gentleman and introduce myself. My name is Giuseppe Daleo, at your service, Miss."

Reaching her house at the top of the hill, Andrea's memory of meeting Giu faded. Storming through the front door, she covered her face, tears poured through her fingers, and flew past her mother. Maria's eyes widened in disbelief as she turned to see her agitated daughter running through the kitchen. She had never seen her cheerful child so distraught. As she turned to follow Andrea, her husband, somewhere between angry and annoyed at himself for making his precious girl cry, stomped into the kitchen.

Maria stopped and spun around.

"Ah, Vincenzo, what did you say to her?"

"I told her what you should have told her weeks ago. Giu Daleo is turning her head. You are her mother. You should know what this could mean," pausing a moment to get control of himself, Vincenzo continued through clenched teeth, "a disgrace to our family."

"Vincenzo, can't you see she is just infatuated with him? He's witty and charming. She's a good girl, so there's no reason to worry."

Controlling her response, Maria ended the discussion with an abrupt turn on her heels. She was tired of Vincenzo's dominance over everything in their lives, especially his rule over Andrea.

Vincenzo was the eldest of five brothers and very much used to being heard and having his say. Three of his brothers worked for him, and out of habit and the fact that he was the oldest, respected him and followed his advice and his lead. His commanding nature made it clear he believed there was strength in numbers and going off searching for another life was a sure way to bleed the family's strength.

Sadly, a fourth brother had drowned in a fishing accident off the coast of Naples when he was a young man. His death left a huge gap in all of the brothers' hearts, but it also brought them closer together. It was a strong family and Vincenzo intended to have it remain that way. Giuseppe Daleo wasn't going to upset his apple cart.

Moving past the morning discord, Andrea went on with her day until the sun set into the dusty southern sky, and the family returned home to enjoy a hearty supper at Maria's table. The morning's conflict didn't carry over to the evening meal, as Vincenzo was clear that meals were for bonding, not for disagreements.

The family sat together for a generous feast, starting off with escarole soup, and then Maria's specialty, handmade *fusilli* pasta served with fried meatballs and sweet, home-made sausage. Typical of the family's dynamics, everyone spoke at once and mouthed each morsel with chunks of freshly baked bread dipped in thick, red, tomato sauce.

Tonight, over the final course of salad fresh from Maria's garden, Vincenzo cracked open a hazelnut as he appraised his family and his home. He loved his wife dearly. She had been his strength through many hard times. They were now wealthy in many ways; they lived well and were respected in their village. After their first years in a tiny apartment, the wine business provided enough to buy this house. It was better than most, at the top of a winding road by the quiet end of town. The rustic, sepia walls were faded with age, but glowed against the blue of the southern sky. He was proud of his home and loved that his wife's focus was on their family. Maria made sure the house welcomed all with front steps flanked by overflowing flowerpots that she replanted with the change of the seasons.

Across the table, Maria witnessed the sadness in her daughter's face and pondered her own thoughts. Her mother-in-law, Angela, had lived with them for years and did what she could to contribute to the family. Mostly, she'd watched over her grandchildren from the day they were born. She was the one who coached Maria as she gave birth to each child. Over the years, they'd become close like mother and daughter. It had always been clear to Maria that of all her children, Angela loved Andrea the most. Maybe it was because she was the only girl, or maybe because Angela saw herself in her vivacious granddaughter.

The pain from Angela's passing only six months before was still raw for Maria. In the midst of the supper chatter, Maria closed her eyes in remembrance of their final night together.

The evening was eerily quiet...Angela was lingering, holding on to life by a thread. With great difficulty, she lifted herself off the pillows that I had lovingly stacked. The tension between Vincenzo and Andrea had had been building for weeks and had obviously reached Angela. Softly cupping my hands in hers, she spoke in carefully chosen words.

"Remember Maria, protect your daughter from the rule of others. Let her find her own love and her own life. My son is a good man, but he sees the world as a place he can control, and it seems he's attempting to extend his dominance over Andrea. She has a spirit that should not be broken."

I sighed that I understood and patted Angela's hand in response. "Yes, Mama Angela, I will try." Holding Angela's hand, and praying, I watched my insightful mother-in-law slip away.

Were those words of wisdom or words of warning from my dying mother-in-law? I know from my own experience it's not easy being a woman in a man's world. Even though Vincenzo is a controlling man, we have a good marriage, but I know that isn't always the case. I only hope I have the courage to follow Angela's advice to give my daughter the gift of choice, but hoping doesn't always make it so.

Even though she was surrounded by family at her kitchen table, Maria shivered from the wind that suddenly blew in through the open window and chilled the night air.

Their five children had been born in this house on the bed where they were conceived. With each birth, Maria was brave and silent. She bore Vincenzo III, who everyone called Terzo, named after her husband and the grandfather before him. He was grown now and a source of pride. He and his new wife lived in a quaint cottage on the other side of the vineyard. Several mornings a week he'd climb the hill with his father and join his siblings for breakfast. On those mornings, Maria was the happiest.

Antonio was a spitting image of his mother, but his perceptions and ways were just as solidly old world as his fathers. They were best of friends and spent many a evening after dinner together at the street cafe in town. Leaving their homes and children to their wives, they'd take a little time to drink anisette and smoke cigars in the coolness of the night.

Alesandro was the third in line. He was born a weak child, not as strong as Terzo or as dashing as Antonio. Antonio had charmed the church school nuns with his smile, but this son always surprised them with his intelligence. Now, as an adult, he oversaw the sales at the family winery. He sold across Italy, making deals with the shippers in Naples and up and down the coast.

The youngest, Luca, was not able to find his place in life. He helped supervise the warehouse, but didn't love the work. Even with his lovely sweetheart, Ana, Luca just couldn't settle down. Weekends he'd catch a ride on the new train into Naples and stay with his friend, Gino, who had already moved from his family's home in the countryside to the city.

*

Luca met Gino on a Saturday night in June two years earlier. At twenty-two, he was a party boy and spent many weekends with Gino at the seaside bars at the port of Naples.

One evening, trying to be a ladies' man, he approached the flirting girlfriend of a local sailor and lazily rubbed his hand down her back as he bent to kiss her neck. After too much wine and not enough experience to know she was playing a game with him, he woke up on his back just outside the bar on the wooden sidewalk with, luckily, only a bloody nose. The girl's boyfriend saw to it that he ended Luca's advances with one swift punch and a kick out the side door of the local hangout.

Finally, opening his eyes, Luca found Gino leaning over him, grinning from ear to ear.

"Hey, buddy, you ought to know about Carmelita. Her old man thinks she's a saint. She has a habit of convincing him that she never looks at anyone else, until she does. You must be new around here."

Luca reached up and took the friendly stranger's out-stretched hand. Once standing, he leaned against the stone wall, his head spinning from the wine and the punch.

"Hey, by the way, I'm Gino. Why don't you come to my apartment and clean up? I live alone, and it wouldn't be a bother. Anyway, any guy who is crazy enough to walk into this part of town and act like he owns the place is my kind of guy."

With this chance meeting, Luca and Gino became tight friends. It was Gino's one room apartment above the butcher's shop that Luca ran to on weekends.

Because this was a week night, Luca was home for supper. He wasn't so preoccupied with his young life that he couldn't see

Andrea was not herself. There had been a child, a girl, born after Luca, but she hadn't lived past eight months. He remembered that prayers to God didn't save the child. Even though Luca was very young at the time, it made such an impression on him that he treasured this sister even more. Luca silently proclaimed himself her protector, so he made a mental note to find out what it was that had her so upset.

Vincenzo slowly cracked open another hazelnut and added the shell to the pile he'd been making since his last bite of fruit. His eyes passed over each member of his family as they sat around the dinner table chatting about the day's events. His gaze stopped on Luca.

I'm not pleased with Luca's shenanigans, but I hope if he has a chance to sow his oats, he'll eventually settle down and be happy with his girlfriend, Ana, and the family business.

Next, his eyes focused on Andrea. Noticing she was unusually silent, his thoughts drifted back to the morning squabble.

My heart hurts for the words we had over the Daleo boy, but I know no other way...not used to being disobeyed...can't bear disgrace for my precious girl or this family. Hmmm...maybe the time has come...arrange a courtship for my sweet daughter...old friend...Mario Salvino...son, Marco...hmmm...already an important part of his father's cheese business. Best mozzarella in the region...Marco has a good future. The more I think about it...Marco is a perfect match for Andrea.

As he rose from the table for his nightly stroll to the cafe, he decided now was the time to take control of his daughter's future.

Chapter 14
The Marriage Plan
Andra' tutto bene, vedrai.
(Everything will be fine, you'll see.)

Vincenzo had no intention of letting his wife handle the situation with Andrea.

She's too soft with this child. Giu Daleo is not going to get a chance to dirty my daughter's name. It's clear...Andrea is mesmerized by this man...can't let it go on for a minute more. Too much grief with the Daleos...with Giu back in town...I don't need more aggravation.

Walking along a quiet alley on his way to meet his good friend, Marino Salvino, he stopped at a bend in the path, contemplating his next move. Staring up at the starlit sky, the turbulent story of the Daleos came roaring back to him.

Ten years before, not sure what to do to help Teresa Daleo after he had no choice but to fire her husband, Ernesto, Vincenzo had asked Marino for his opinion.

"Marino, unfortunately Ernesto Daleo has been

drinking for quite a long while, which has caused many issues at the winery. He's either not showing up for work or coming in hung over. There's no question his behavior has now affected more than his work. I've kept him on out of compassion for his family, but I was finally forced to fire him."

Marino knew the difficulties of raising a family and could only imagine the burden put on Ernesto's wife, Teresa. After pondering how serious the situation was for the Daleo family, he suggested Vincenzo speak with the parish priest.

"Vincenzo, it's not uncommon for Father Falchi to get involved in the lives of the town's people. He's helped many families through hard times, so maybe he can offer some assistance with the Daleos now"

"Marino. I think you might be right. The church is a good place to start. I can't stop Ernesto's drinking, but maybe with Father Falchi's assistance we can find a way to help the family."

Following his friend's advice, Vincenzo made his way to Saint Matthew's. The stone and mortar church sat on Via Nicola on the Southeast side of town just after the houses thinned out and rolling, green hills began. The church's cross barely towered over the bell tower, but it still guided the villagers to Piazza Nicola where all the Catholic festivities were celebrated. If it was Christmas, the nativity was set up in the center of the piazza for all to see. If it was Easter, the fresh lilies lined the stone steps that led to the church portico. Every season and every occasion, joyous or sad, started and ended at these doors.

Vincenzo opened the heavy, wooden door and entered the silent church. The air was cool compared to the afternoon sun, and the scent of sage incense lingered from yesterday's Sunday mass. The echo of Vincenzo's steps alerted Father Falchi who was just rising from his afternoon prayers. A smile crossed his face when he saw Vincenzo. He'd watched him grow from an altar boy who served Sunday mass into a honored family man, and he knew the goodness of his heart. After greetings and a few minutes of catching up on the Parrish news, Father Falchi motioned for Vincenzo to sit with him in the front pew.

"So, my friend, what has brought you here today?" He could sense that something was disturbing Vincenzo and hoped there was something he could do to help.

"Father, I'm not here to meddle, but I feel I have some responsibility in the matter, so I feel I must reach out for assistance."

Father Falchi's stomach turned with trepidation hoping Vincenzo hadn't gotten himself in a bind. "Yes, my son, please go on."

Letting out a deep breath, Vincenzo began his story.

"You know the Daleo family, in particular Ernesto Daleo. He worked for me, but I had to let him go. You see, he'd been drinking for a long time and not doing his work. I tried to overlook his poor performance at work, actually no performance. He's been coming in smelling like booze and falling asleep on the job.

"Anyway, several Saturdays ago, I was at the market and overheard his wife, Teresa, trying to buy groceries without money. She was pretty much begging the fishmonger to give her the fare on credit while promising to come back to pay him by the following Saturday. I had just paid her husband his weekly salary at the end of the day on Friday, so it made no sense that she had no money for food by Saturday afternoon.

"Then, the following week, Ernesto didn't show for work until Friday, obviously for his pay. I explained that his drinking and his countless days absent, plus the complaints brought to me by my brothers, gave me no choice but to fire him.

"Needless to say, it didn't end well, and now I'm worried for Teresa and her three children. I've considered reaching out to her oldest son, Francesco, to explain the situation and without embarrassing him, offer him a job. I know he's been looking for work and being the eldest he may want to take on some responsibility and give his mom a hand. However, I'm not sure how he would react to an offer from me with all that's happened."

It wasn't the first time the priest had heard similar stories. Over the years there were many heartaches that his parishioners endured, with one of the most common coming from an issue with alcohol.

"How can I help, Vincenzo? My avenues are limited, but I will do whatever I can. I see Teresa at Sunday mass, and thinking about it now, lately, she seems to have avoided stopping by to say hello on her way out after mass. I didn't think much about it, because she's always collecting her children to scurry home, but now I understand. She's carrying a great deal on her shoulders, and being embarrassed, she must not know where to turn."

"Well, Father, I know when my wife, Maria, comes to help with the church fairs, she, and please do not let me embarrass you, always says it would be so nice if you had someone to help you here at the parish. You have so many responsibilities with the parishioners and the school, as well as officiating baptisms, marriages and funerals. You even oversee the church cemetery. As you know, Teresa is known for her wonderful cooking and always brought the best zeppole to sell at the church fairs.

"The next fair is coming up in two weeks, and we were thinking that you might want to compliment Teresa on her delicious baking and suggest it would be so nice if you had someone to help out at the parish house. Without her knowing we ever spoke, you'd be offering her part-time work that might help her get by."

For an extended moment, Father Falchi said nothing. Vincenzo worried he had stepped over the line with the priest. He started to apologize for being so presumptuous, but was stopped by the priest's upheld hand.

"It's been a long time since I've had help here. Since Mrs. Rosa passed away, I've never given replacing her much thought. Rightfully so, I could use the help. The parish would benefit if I could focus more time on my parishioners and less time on the everyday chores."

Vincenzo took a deep breath, and his look of relief brought a smile to the Father's face. Things played out with Father Falchi's help, just as Marino had suggested. At the next fair, Teresa took her place in the church basement in charge of the pizza fritte sales. With hundreds of pounds of flour and fifteen women from the parish to help, she oversaw one of the biggest church fund raisers of the year. There was no question she had organizational skills in addition to her baking talents. Her success provided Father Falchi with the perfect opportunity to offer her a job, and Teresa willingly accepted.

Pushing the prior Daleo troubles out of his thoughts, Vincenzo focused on the Daleo issue at hand, as he continued his walk to the village cafe contemplating his proposal for Marino. Watching the smoke from his cigar curl above his head and drift into the night, he realized even though he'd helped

Teresa, the one thing he could never repair was the damage to Teresa's youngest son, Giu, who as an angry teenager left Sicignano and his family behind.

Approaching the lit torches marking the cafe grounds, Vincenzo waved to Marino who was already sitting at a table in the distance. His deep, hearty laugh floated through the night air putting a smile on Vincenzo's face. He loved this man as any man could love another. They'd been friends since childhood growing up in the hills of Campania. Marino was as wiry as he'd always been. He could never sit still. His hands spoke his words as fast as his mouth, and he was always tapping out a song with his foot. He'd grown, like Vincenzo, into a respected family man. As Terzo's godfather, Marino stood proudly holding Vincenzo's first born at the church Christening as Father Falchi prayed and poured holy water over the child's forehead. Together they'd shared hardships and joys, and a marriage between their children would complete the bond. Vincenzo would have liked nothing better than to make a match for Andrea with Marino's son, Marco.

"Hey, *paisano*, I saw your cheese carts start down the hill today. They were loaded more than usual. You must have enough orders to feed the whole southern coast!" Vincenzo loved to kid Marino. "If you keep the orders this large, you'll be a rich man. Will you still talk to this poor, wine maker?"

Marino laughed. "Look who's talking. Your wines are sold from Rome to Palermo now. If the Sicilians will drink your wine, then for sure you are the one who will be the rich man."

Vincenzo eased into his favorite chair at the cafe table. Years of friendship had left the men comfortable with each other as each knew the other well. However, tonight, even though his friend had goaded him as usual, Marino noticed something wasn't right. Vincenzo's jaw was tight, and his eyes were missing their usual glitter. The fine lines from years in the vineyard's sun somehow seemed deeper tonight. Marino knew if he waited, Vincenzo would eventually share what was on his mind.

Vincenzo tossed the last inch of wine down and waved to the waiter for another glass.

"Marino, you remember the Daleos, don't you?"

"Yes, of course, I haven't forgotten how you tried to repair the damage Ernesto caused."

"Well, his son, Giu, has returned, and the Daleos are once again bringing grief to my family."

With a deep sigh, Vincenzo shared the details and his concerns about Andrea's attraction for Giu.

"Marino, you know my daughter, she's a beautiful girl with so much to offer. And, your son, Marco, is such an amazing young man with a wonderful future. I think I have a solution that will benefit both of our families."

At first, Vincenzo's plan had focused on making the Daleos go away, until he realized it did so much more. It would bind Marino's family together with his forever. Pleased with his strategy, Vincenzo proposed a marriage between their children. It was a perfect match, Marco, and Andrea.

Marino's reaction was instant. He'd also been tossing around ideas for his son's future. Marco didn't have a girlfriend, and it was about time he settled down. The timing for both families was ideal. With a handshake and a clink of their glasses, the two friends agreed it was a splendid plan.

Raising their glasses to the heavens, they shouted in unison.

"Salute! May God bless the future union of our children!"

Chapter 15
The Daleos
Non tutte le ciambelle riescono col buco
(Things don't always turn out as planned)

Giuseppe Daleo, known as Giu to his family and school-mates, left Sicignano degli Alburni when he was 17. He'd grown up in a rickety, old structure perched on the edge of a ridge. He remembered poverty as a child. His mother, Teresa, had taken in wash and for years tried to make enough money to subsidize his father's pay. His old man drank too much. That's all there was to it. He couldn't hold a job and the burden of sustaining the family fell more and more on Teresa. Teresa tried to do little things just for Giu, since he was the youngest, but it was impossible to do much with three children under her care. With flour and water, she'd knead balls of dough and let them rise near the heat of the kitchen stove. When she had enough oil and sugar left over from what she needed for the week, she'd stretch the dough and pop each into a pan of hot oil. Once golden, she'd let Giu toss the fried balls in sweet, white sugar. Giu felt so special on those mornings warmed by the stove eating his mother's *pizza fritte.*

Their house was built on the edge of a hill. It had been the caretaker's house on the grounds belonging to a wealthy family. The family had long since moved, their main house falling to ruin after a fire and a downturn in their financial status. The years took their toll on the caretaker's house, and it stood abandoned with no one claiming the old structure, until Ernesto usurped the homestead and moved his family into the shabby abode. As a little child, Giu spent hours peeking through the separated floorboards in his shared bedroom, looking onto the valley below. Imagining he could squeeze through the slats and soar away like a bird, he'd daydream his worries away and pretend he was far from the poverty and discord that permeated his house.

Unlike Giu, Teresa no longer envisioned a future any different from her present. She did her best to make their hovel a home, but there was just so much one woman could do.

In the beginning, Teresa was in love. Ernesto didn't live in her village. She wasn't sure, but she thought he came from a seaside town south of Salerno. One April evening, Teresa met him at a church feast. Every April seventh, the parishioners gathered to honor and celebrate their patron, Saint Matthew. Enjoying the evening, Teresa giggled with her girlfriends, each teasing the other to see who would have the courage to go on the church stage and sing a Neapolitan song. Every year, there was a contest for the most beautiful voice in Sicignano. With a push from her best friend, Nicola, she stumbled up the stage steps. She stood there with the statue of Saint Matthew as Father Falchi and a crowd stared at her. With no choice but to sing, she muttered to the local musician and took her place at the front of the stage. Hesitant, almost whispering, she sang the first few lines of the popular Neapolitan Tarantella. *Gialaluna è in mezzo al mare, Mamma Mia ...*

One by one, the people in the square turned away from their joking and laughing. As the din of the crowd slowly quieted to her beautiful voice, Teresa's confidence grew. Raising her voice and swaying her hips, she began twirling and weaving across the stage. The crowd went wild, swinging and intertwining in each other's arms. The atmosphere was exhilarating. The church musician played faster and louder and the crowd got lost in their own revery.

Just at that moment, an arm slipped through hers and a young man swung her around as she belted out her song. She hadn't seen him climb onto the stage. No matter, with the excitement of the moment, she sang and danced along to exhaustion. When she caught her breath, rosy-cheeked from the heat of the night, she found herself being applauded by the crowd, but the young man was nowhere to be seen.

Once off the stage, her friends hugged and kissed her, as they all laughed together, but Teresa was preoccupied and kept searching the crowd.

Who was that handsome young man? Where has he gone?

She eyed the congregation for the rest of the night but couldn't find the stranger anywhere.

At the end of the festivities, Teresa and her friends walked home together following the winding streets. One by one they said goodnight, as they each reached their house, until Teresa found herself alone climbing the path to her front door.

"That was some song and dance." A deep, dark voice came to her from around the bend by the bougainvillea tree.

Startled, she stopped and twisted around to run back down the path.

"No, please don't go. It's me. The very same young man you just whirled around the stage."

Teresa froze. There he was, standing in the moonlight with a soft smile curved on his amused face. She'd dreamt of meeting a prince just like the *Principessa* in all those tales, but never believed it was a reality. Struck by Ernesto's suave, good looks and beaming smile, she coyly acknowledged her prince.

"Really? As I recall, you were twirling me."

Teresa knew nothing about Ernesto. When he showed up the night of Saint Matthew's feast, he came with no explanation. She never learned much more about his life than what he was willing to share, which in the end wasn't much. Paying it no mind, in the weeks that passed, she only thought of him and spent every free minute meeting him whenever she could get away. Teresa knew her parents would not approve, but that didn't stop her. At 17 she believed she knew what she was doing, so she concealed their encounters. They'd climb the grassy hillsides together and laugh in the sunshine of lazy afternoons. Ernesto brought local wine, and Teresa secretly slipped food out of her family's kitchen wrapped in a large towel. It was heaven. On hot days, they'd find their way to the river and dip in the cool, moving water. When he finally kissed her, she felt her whole world come together.

Weeks passed, and as happy as she was, she still knew nothing about him. One day, she tried to ask him about his family and his life, but Ernesto pulled away with an angry frown, his smile gone. She couldn't stand to look at him so upset, so she begged him to forgive her. With a few kisses to his neck, she managed to get him to come around. She quickly learned to leave his story alone. It really didn't matter, because he made her happy. She loved him and couldn't imagine being without him. So, when he asked her to marry him, without a second thought, she said yes over and over again.

A few years after their third child was born, things changed. Ernesto wasn't just drinking to relax anymore. He was drinking to live. Teresa struggled with Ernesto's drinking and did her best to encourage him stop, but nothing she said made a difference. It was like they were riding on a runaway cart. Teresa just didn't know when they would finally crash. As time passed, they ended up living in an old caretaker's house with not much of anything to their name. Their only treasure was their children. In four short years of marriage, she'd given birth to three children. Francesco was the first, then Isabella, and the last Giuseppe.

Giuseppe was ten years old when his father's drinking became so problematic that he'd been fired from his job at the Fiorano winery. Vincenzo had tolerated Ernesto's behavior for many years. Knowing Teresa was struggling to raise three children brought out the compassion in him, so he kept Ernesto on the job.

At first, Ernesto worked hard. Then, after a while, he started showing up late several mornings a week to his job in the vat rooms. The cellar manager would find him, more often than not, sleeping in the corner with his head against an empty wine barrel, oblivious to the rest of the workers. Vincenzo's brothers, repeatedly told Vincenzo to get rid of Ernesto, but he kept him on. Vincenzo had many talks with Ernesto, and each time Ernesto would promise to stop drinking and straighten out. He'd smile and talk about his beautiful wife and his wonderful children and go on about how important they were to him. As time went by, he didn't stop drinking, but due to Vincenzo's good graces, he still got his pay every Friday afternoon. Vincenzo supposed that by not firing him, he was providing a much-needed income for the man's family.

One Saturday morning, Vincenzo was at the open-air market, picking up fresh produce and searching for purple figs for Maria. She loved the sweet, plump fruit wrapped in purple tissue paper, and he loved to pamper her, so he'd buy the whole box to take home for Sunday dinner.

Opening shop in the last hours of dawn, the venders started their day. With barely any morning light, the booths were set up early each Saturday. Before the customers came to peruse the goods, the merchants drank their morning coffee, frothing with warm milk mixed in the same bowl they'd used for years. All the market people knew each other, so after shouting a few friendly exchanges, the day would begin. The market quickly busied as the townspeople called out their orders, while mongers sold fresh fish and farmers touted colorful vegetables from the local fields. Vendors yelled out their prices and local matrons argued over the cost. The morning sun getting brighter each moment, rose over the wooden pushcarts, and the smells and voices blended into a lively racket.

While searching for the figs, Vincenzo shuffled a mound of prickly pears around the fruit cart, looking for the ones ripe and soft enough to eat, when he smelled the aroma of roasting chestnuts. Enticed by a whiff of the organic smell, he put the juicy pear back on the pile and came around to the chestnut cart. This was the first harvest of the year, and he knew his family would love to eat them after dinner, while they sat by the light of the fireplace. As he shifted through the now cramped aisles, he heard Teresa Dalco's voice. He stopped behind strings of hanging bulbs of garlic and dried red peppers tied to a wooden pole. He caught a glimpse of the side of her face, but she couldn't detect his presence. Her pleading voice was what had caught his attention.

"Please Signore. One more week and I will make good on my bill. My family needs to eat. Some fish, just this week, and I will pay you in full next Saturday."

Vincenzo questioned himself.

How can this be? I just paid her husband his weekly wages yesterday afternoon. How can his wife already be without money for food? I'm keeping a drunk on my payroll for the sake of the family, and he's drinking his pay away!

He quickly came up behind Teresa, so she wouldn't realize he had overheard any of her conversation. He greeted her politely, and in doing so with his eyes told the fish man to fill her request. Understanding the signal, the fishmonger, knowing Vincenzo for many years and knowing his well-respected reputation, asked Teresa how many kilos she wanted. A little confused, but oblivious to their silent communication, she nervously answered the monger, quickly took the paper-wrapped goods, offered her good day and disappeared into the crowd. What Vincenzo didn't know was Giu, Ernesto and Teresa's ten-year-old son, was standing across the way behind stacked tomato crates, and he had heard and seen everything.

By the end of the following week, Vincenzo knew what he had to do. He had no choice but to fire Giu's father. Vincenzo was uncomfortable letting Ernesto go, but there was no point in keeping him employed when his family wasn't benefitting from his earnings.

Ernesto hadn't bothered to show up all week, until Friday, obviously for his pay with no real intention of working. Knowing something was up when the foreman told him the boss wanted to see him, and only slightly inebriated with a vague odor of liquor emanating from his pores, Ernesto arrogantly pushed Vincenzo's office door open. Vincenzo calmly explained to Ernesto that he was being let go because of his countless days absent and because of numerous complaints from the floor supervisors.

Slurring his words, he insulted Vincenzo. "You son-of-a-bitch. You used me. When you needed a man with experience in the vats, I was okay. You paid me piss money. My family couldn't even live on it, and now because I've been a little sick, you let me go with a wife and three children to feed."

There was only one bit of truth in his empty insults. No one knew anything about Ernesto when he first came to town. Teresa was not alone in her curiosity about his past. But his charm and gentlemanly behavior had won over, and he'd been accepted by her family and the town's people. When Ernesto had come to the winery for a job, Vincenzo sat with him and talked about the business and together they'd walked through the wine cellar. By the end of the interview, he realized Ernesto knew something about winemaking and offered him a job. No one ever did find out much more about him than at some time he had worked with the vines.

Ernesto's voice grew louder, and he pounded his fist on the office desk. Enraged, his eyes turned bloodshot. Antonio, hearing the commotion in his father's office, rushed through the door just as Ernesto moved around the desk and took a swing at Vincenzo's face. Vincenzo stepped back just as Antonio grabbed Ernesto from behind. Witnessing the scene through the office glass, Vincenzo's youngest brother came running and together they spun Ernesto around and pushed him out the office door into the bright day light. He continued yelling and throwing his arms around, cursing and threatening the whole family, but he wasn't done. As he stepped forward to punch Antonio, Terzo came around the corner, stepped between them and pushed him back into the dirt road.

Unhappy with the whole situation, the Fioranos turned to go back inside the office. None of them noticed that Giu, Ernesto's ten-year-old son, was again watching from the side of the road. He'd seen his father pushed into the dirt knowing nothing of the argument Ernesto had started inside. Hiding his embarrassed for his father, he pulled back behind a tree and waited. His father staggered to stand, swearing insults as he brushed the road dust from his work clothes.

That night Giu witnessed a stormy quarrel between his parent's. His father blamed everything on the Fioranos. When Teresa accused him of being an alcoholic, he raised his hand to quiet her and tripping forward hit her in the face. Intentional or not, his wedding ring scrapped across her lip cutting into her soft skin. She clasped her hands over her bleeding mouth and retreated, frightened by the assault and embarrassed that her children had been witness to the scene. Her lip, red and swelling, she hurried the children into the one small bedroom they shared. The scene scarred Gio. He was so emotionally torn, wanting to love his father, the father he remembered as a toddler who tossed peanuts in the air for him to catch in his mouth. But those memories were long vague, and the most recent so ugly. Then, thinking like a ten-year-old, he decided maybe his father was right.

Those Fioranos ruined my father's life. Yes, that's it. Everything was fine before my father started to work for that family. My whole life is ruined because of those people. Those sons of bitches. Who do they think they are? Treating my mother with pity at the fish market and throwing my father into the road. Now, see what's happened. My father hit my mother because of them.

The commotion from his parent's final argument finally calmed down, but then he heard the front door slam off its hinges. Peeking out the bedroom door, he saw his father leaving as the door bounced back open from the force of the slam. Giu heard his mother finally speak up. She was yelling at Ernesto as the door banged back in her face.

"And don't come back. You are nothing but a drunk."

That was the last time Giu ever saw his father. That night, Ernesto left Sicignano for good, and his son knew who was to blame.

Chapter 16
Marco's Secret
In vino veritas
(In wine there is truth)

After the morning argument he'd had with Andrea for meeting with Giu Daleo, Vincenzo was sure his daughter would follow his wishes. She wouldn't disobey him. Besides, once she accepted Marco's engagement, he was certain the Daleo issue would be history. In fact, Andrea never mentioned Giu again. Vincenzo believed he had accomplished his quest to remove Giu from his daughter's life, as well as to match her with Marco Salvino. He knew it was the right thing to do, and in the end, he felt love and family won out.

Marco Salvino was such a good catch and wasn't romantically involved with any of the girls in the village. When Vincenzo approached Marino about his plan for their children, Marino had agreed it would be a splendid idea and such wonderful bond for the families. Their two children, what could be better?

However, even though Andrea and Marco knew each other since childhood, they hadn't had a connection except when the families celebrated Christmas or birthdays together. Andrea went to the all-girls Catholic school attached to Saint Matthews, while Marco, two years ahead, went to the local agricultural, trade school with plans to one day take over his father's cheese business. So, on the tenth of June, Andrea's eighteenth birthday, the fathers' plan unfolded. Vincenzo was to throw a fabulous birthday party for Andrea. Marino asked Marco, who was known for his singing voice, to sing *Tanti Auguri* as a birthday surprise. Ever since Marco was an altar boy, he'd sung in the church choir. Every Sunday morning, above all the others, his voice filled the church. It would not be unusual for him to sing a birthday song to Andrea.

The birthday plan went well. Andrea laughed and clapped listening to Marco lead the celebration. They left the stage with Marco's arm wrapped around Andrea's shoulder, and for the rest of the evening, they were seen chatting with a group of Andrea's friends. It seemed the two fell in together as if they were made for each other.

Months went by when Marino concluded it was time to have a serious conversation with his son about his intentions with Andrea. Marco's response was so clear. He told his father that he and Andrea had become the best of friends. He shared that they had so much in common and so many laughs. Marino heard what he wanted to hear and considered what he heard as good news. So, he pressed his son to take the next step. After a speech about the respectful thing to do before there were any embarrassing incidents and his responsibilities now as the junior leader of the cheese company, Marino persuaded Marco to ask Andrea to marry him. Marco wasn't used to refusing his father, and he did like Andrea, but only as a friend. He tried to stress that fact with his father, but it fell on deaf ears. Not knowing much about romance and after his father's encouragement, Marco convinced himself that in time, Andrea would fall in love with him, and he with her. They were young with many years to fall in love.

However, there was that other thing. For years Marco believed if he ignored it, it would eventually go away. Marco liked being an altar boy. The real truth was as a child and young teen, Marco liked the other altar boys. Ever since he could remember, he found a warmth around the other boys that he never felt around the girls. When they wrestled on the hill behind the church, he liked the boy's touches. Marco longed for Saturday mornings when the choir boys gathered behind the altar playing around teasing each other before they'd march up to the choir loft and practice songs for the Sunday mass. He loved every minute of those Saturdays and Sundays, but knowing there was no way he could share his feelings with anyone, especially his father, he said nothing.

When Marco reached school age, Marino enrolled him in an all-boys agricultural school. Marino believed the school's training was necessary to make his son into the man he needed to be to run the family business. Many fathers and grandfathers, like Marco's father, had worked for years to build up their olive oil and cheese trades. They each looked forward to when their sons would be able to oversee the field workers, sell their products and help their families take the businesses to the next level. Times were changing, and the old guard was looking to the future.

Each year, the school principal arranged for the boys

with the best grades to take a field trip, to experience how successful businesses were operated throughout Italy. A family-run olive farm, which was known across Italy for its oil, had olive groves that ran for miles in every direction, and the family had become very wealthy selling oil. Marco, never being away from home without his family, was excited when he was one of the boys chosen for the weekend field trip. The plan to take the new train from the country to the coast was finalized, and the eight boys along with the upper-level teacher were set to go.

The train jerked and swayed through the hills and the rolling mountain passes until it came out of a tunnel with a view of the glorious sea in the distance. As they sped closer to the shore, groves of thick, irregularly, twisted trees came into view. The whitish underside of the leaves gave the impression of pale green snow. Nets were spread like spider webs along the hills, catching the loose olives to prevent them from cascading into the ravines and roads below.

When the train pulled into the station, they were greeted by bright, blue skies and bountiful bougainvillea. The professor collected the boys, and carrying their satchels, they followed him the short distance to the grove. The boys were directed to a long, wooden building flanking the first row of olive trees. The interior was divided into four, small rooms, and two boys were assigned to bunk together in each. The professor was invited into the main house as an honored guest of the owners.

Exhausted and hungry, the boys were relieved to see a long, wooden table set out under the trees laden with sausages, an assortment of cheese, and stacks of warm bread. There were bowls of fresh olives and oils for dipping, along with plates of grapes. Feeling very welcome, the boys grabbed for the food and stuffed their mouths to feed their hungry stomachs. Liking the looks of Rose, the kitchen girl, who was setting up the feast, and finally feeling free being so far from home, they began flirting with her. They chimed in together, complementing her pretty face while they were really gawking at her robust breasts. Rose was as happy as could be in the groves with these new boys who were almost her age. She let them flirt, and when she turned away, she quickly unbuttoned the top button of her dress, so a bit more of her white breast could show. She was loving the attention, being so bored with the local boys. Thinking she could really be a hit if she could give them something more, she returned from the kitchen with a jug of wine under each arm. Growing up, the boys drank a bit of wine with their families at dinner, but not out of jugs in the night in an olive grove with a beautiful girl with breasts.

No one came to check on them. The professor was a distance away, and no one from the farm was anywhere near the groves, except Rose. She sat on the lap of the oldest-looking boy while he squeezed her waist and whispered in her ear. The rest of the boys laughed and joked and took quick looks at Rose as they managed to drink both jugs.

Wanting the revelry to last into the night, Rose got off her boy's lap and returned with two more jugs which the already inebriated schoolboys did not refuse. Slapping each other on the back and swaying back and forth as they sang their school song, they were looser than they'd ever had a chance to be. Not wanting the night to end, but finally exhausted from the day's travel and the overdose of wine and food, one by one the boys made their way to their bunks. Rose took her boy by the hand and led him around the kitchen to the room she slept in on the nights she stayed late working at the grove.

Marco had been watching Rose with his school friend and wondered what it must feel like to be touched like that. Marco didn't want to be obvious, but when he could, he'd sneak a peek at the two lovebirds. It looked like Rose was moving back and forth on the boy's lap while both were intent on each other's eyes. By the time Rose and the boy got up to leave, the boy's hand was brazenly cupping Rose's pale, white breast inside her unbuttoned blouse.

Tipsy and aroused, Marco wandered to his bunk. The bunks must have been old stables for the goats. Sometime in the past, they'd been cleaned up, painted and partitioned into separate rooms for the grove workers with sleeping quarters pressed up two per room. Each old stall was separated from the rest with a door, and each had two wooden platforms with mattresses lined up against each other. When Marco opened the door to his room, his bunk partner was already getting undressed. Marco walked in just as the boy took off his pants and turned toward the door. Totally drunk, the boy stood buck naked, facing Marco.

"Hey, Marco, some night tonight! What did you think of that Rose? Too bad we all couldn't get some tonight."

All the years of desire, too much wine, and watching Rose push her buttocks down on the boy's lap was more than Marco could handle. He moved toward the boy slowly, removing his shirt first, and then one leg of his pants at a time without ever taking his eyes off the boy. He was also drunk and now naked. As he moved closer, the boy looked into his eyes.

"Yes," Marco whispered, "it's too bad we all couldn't get some of that tonight."

That night was heaven and hell for Marco. In the morning light, he couldn't look at the boy. Both were naked on one bunk. Marco hurried to get dressed before anyone discovered them. He spent the next day with the group staying as far away from the boy as he could.

It was mid-November, harvest time, so the boys were

given rakes to experience harvesting the low-hanging purple fruit. With one hand, they'd bunch up several branches while using the rake to carefully brush the olives into nets. Every once and awhile, Marco noticed the boy frantically looking his way, as if he wanted to say something, but Marco wouldn't give him a chance. He kept busy, first raking, then gathering the olives into crates.

There was one more night to sleep in the bunks before they returned home, Marco waited. After the boys finished eating, Rose's boy went off with her again, and one by one the boys headed for their bunks.

I can't bear going to my room. It was an accident. I was drunk. What will my father think if he finds out?

So, that last night, Marco slept under the olive trees and prayed and promised it would never happen again.

The years passed, and Marco tried his best to keep his promise. When his father positioned him with the marriage plan, Marco thought it could possibly be his way out. He remembered that night when he was in the tenth level in the olive grove and remembered Rose. Maybe he could feel like Rose's boy with Andrea. Once married to her, he was sure his love for her would grow, and he wouldn't have to think about what he really wanted.

Chapter 17
As Luck May Have It
Chi trova un amico trova un tesoro
(Who finds a friend finds a treasure)

Against her father's command, Andrea had been secretly seeing Giu. She'd tried to respect her father's wishes, but she couldn't suppress her feelings for Giu. He'd become everything to her. She was captivated by his dark, wavy hair and piercing blue eyes, and the way he held her face when he lifted it for a kiss. They talked for hours, sneaking away to be alone by the river. Her secret place opened into a hill providing a dark, secluded hideaway out of view and perfectly flat for a blanket.

Growing up she'd heard the stories about the feud between Giu's father and her father and the firing. Giu told her he'd witnessed the day her father helped his mother with the fishmonger, as well as the scene when his father was thrown out of the winery's office.

Attempting to explain his previous behavior and to soothe her concerns, Giu shared his story with Andrea.

"Andre, I was only ten years old. I saw what a child

would see. I knew my father was drinking and not being responsible, but at the time I was so angry I didn't want to assign the blame on anyone, except your family. When I left at seventeen, I went off alone, an angry young man."

"Leaving my hilltop home, I found my way up the coast to Naples about seventy miles north. I quickly found a job on a fishing boat that didn't require experience. It wasn't the life I'd planned for myself, but I hadn't really planned anything. It was hard work being out on the sea at night. You see, fishing was only successful on nights with a slight moon and calm ocean. The ocean was full there, unlike other depleted waters, and it gave back as long as we worked hard."

"I found myself working next to tough, sea-weathered men. We'd throw tight mesh-baits into the dark waters and rely on oil lamps to shine light onto the nets to attract the small fish. Once full, we'd dump the catch into the boat and repeat the process all over again. The nights were cold on the open sea, and we were exhausted by our return at dawn. The fishing boats were small and needed only a crew of five or six men, so the men got to know each other. However, being a loner was fine with me at the time, since my resentment had traveled with me from my hometown to the sea. That's until I got to know Agostino."

Andrea, laid back on the soft blanket mesmerized by Giu's voice. "Is Agostino the man you told me about who made such a difference in your life?"

"Yes, he's the man. He was rough around the edges but carried a giving heart. The men called him, Tino. He was the oldest, crankiest fisherman in the crew and the captain of Andiamo. His second marriage fell apart for many reasons, and his wife blamed it on the sea. The truth was Tino had only so much to give. The sea was his salvation and his mistress, so he had nothing left when it was all said and done. He took a liking to me. It wasn't as if I gave him any reason. Rather, it was because he saw himself in me-the angry, young man. When we first met, I'm sure he was convinced I was probably exorcizing my own demons, as he watched me, the newest and youngest of his small crew, work myself to exhaustion. He saw that I communicated with the crew only when necessary. He must have seen his own struggles in me, the tough, ornery kid. He told me later that he had surmised, I'd seen more than my share of the ugly side of life. I was a lucky young man to have found a job on Tino's boat. If I'd been on another captain's boat, I probably wouldn't be sitting here with you today."

Andrea quietly urged Giu to go on. "Please tell me more about your life with Tino in Naples."

"One morning," Giu began, "Andiamo pulled into Porto Santa Lucia, a small port that accommodated the fishing boats and allowed them to dump their catch into ice-packed wooden bins that stood in rows stacked on the docks. It was almost sunrise, and like all fishing harbors, the locals would soon come to buy fish fresh from the sea. I hadn't found a place to sleep in the few weeks I'd been in Naples, nor did I have enough money yet to put up for a room, so each morning I'd hurry off the boat ahead of the other crew to pull my burlap sack out from under the wooden bins before the wet fish from the night's catch was dumped on top.'

"Once we were friends, Tino told me he witnessed my routine for the first time the day before and again that morning, so before I could scurry away, he approached me.

"'Hey, young man,' he said, 'how about getting some food with me? There's a little cafe along the harbor that serves delicious, hot coffee and home-made biscotti. It's perfect for the likes of us.'

"I only had the wages I'd been saving for a room and hadn't been paying for food. Instead, I'd stand out the back side of the harbor restaurants waiting for the leftover kitchen food to be tossed at the end of the night. It was no way to live, but it was keeping me alive."

"Sensing my financial situation, Tino threw his arm around my shoulders. 'Come on, young man. Today's breakfast is on me.'

"While we sipped hot coffee from over-sized mugs, Tino broached the subject of sleeping quarters. He figured I was hard on my luck and could use a place to stay. He kept it light, so as not to scare me away.

"'So, Giu, he said. 'I was married for nine years, no little ones, and everything went to hell. My wife was tired of my nights away at sea and probably'—he wiped his mouth with the back of his hand as he gave a short chuckle—'the smell of fish I brought home every morning. Anyway, she went home to her mother a year ago, and I've been left with an apartment bigger than one man needs. You're new in town. By any chance, are you looking for a place to sleep?'

"I stared across the table at the weathered face. I was young, but not stupid. I searched, looking for a sign that this man was up to no good. All I could find were tired, warm eyes and an honest smile. I'd known him now for a few weeks, and it was clear the crew respected their captain. Truly being in dire straits and trusting my instincts, I looked Tino in the eye and said, 'I won't take a handout. I'll work for my bed and put my money in for food.' I remember looking down at the brown, coffee stain left in my cup, and lifting my head smirking. 'And, I won't put up with your stink either.'

"Tino burst out laughing and reached across the table to shake my hand. 'All right then,' he said. 'It's a goddam deal!'"

Finishing his story, Giu turned to Andrea.

"You see how life works, Andrea. I've changed. I'm not the angry boy your father knew or the young man Tino first met. I'm a better man now because of Tino. There was no way for me to know that early morning as dawn turned to day that a pivotal handshake between two strangers would in so many ways seal my fate and my future. Most of all, because of him, I found my way back home and to you, my love."

Chapter 18
The Denial
Non è tutto oro quello che luccica
(All that glitters is not gold)

The Fioranos were so thrilled to have their only daughter getting married that they invited everyone they knew to the wedding. The guest list stretched from family and friends to every business acquaintance throughout the region. The excitement of the blessed occasion filled the air, as musicians tested and tuned their instruments for the festivities.

On the grounds of the Fiorano winery, Terrabella Wines, a main villa, originally built in the 1700s as a private residence, had been converted into a reception area and a mini hotel for the wine purveyors who came to buy the family's wine. As the Terrabella Wine sales grew, Vincenzo's wife, Maria, suggested they renovate the old villa to raise the presence of the brand. At first, Vincenzo wasn't convinced it was worth the investment, but eventually he took her idea seriously, and in the end, was happy he did. His wine sales had always been good locally, but as the word of the creation of the estate spread, it brought buyers from Naples to Palermo. Tonight, the villa and the grounds would be glowing in candle and torch lights, and the surrounding cypress trees would throw beautiful shadows into the night. It was a magical location for a wedding. Guests were to arrive from the Church of Saint Matthews's, where Father Falchi was going to officiate the wedding vows of Andrea Fiorano and Marco Salvino. The plan was to have family and friends, dressed in their holiday finest, stroll down the hill from the church up the green cypress alleys through wrought-iron gates onto the vineyard grounds. That was the plan.

The sun rose with a special glow and filled the sky with a blaze of pink on the morning of Andrea's wedding to Marco. Vincenzo's excitement kept him from sleeping, so he was up going over his checklist, drinking his morning espresso earlier than usual. Everything was arranged, but he needed to oversee the last-minute details.

Maria woke to find him already in the kitchen, reviewing the wedding plans, starting with the church service and ending with the celebration planned for the villa in the vineyard that night. He wanted to be sure everything was executed to perfection.

Sleeping late on her big day, Andrea finally came down the stairs looking tired and preoccupied. She'd been exceptionally quiet these last weeks. Vincenzo was sure she had a case of wedding jitters and chalked it up to nerves.

"Ah, here she is, my beautiful daughter. What a joyous day. Your mother and I have waited for this moment since you were a little girl, and now it has arrived!"

Vincenzo's excitement filled the air as he greeted Andrea and twirled her around in the middle of the kitchen.

Sensing something was not right with Andrea, Maria hurried Vincenzo out to check the wedding flowers and to double check with the church conductor about the music selected for the choir. She wanted to talk to her daughter alone and needed to get her animated husband out of the house.

Once they were alone in the newfound silence, she turned to her daughter and held her hand as she motioned for her to sit.

"What is it, Andrea? Your wedding is only a few hours away, and you don't look well. Are you all right?"

I'm not even close to all right...don't know how to tell my mother what's wrong. So much time and money has gone into this wedding...my parents are ecstatic over seeing their "little girl" walk down the aisle...sick to my stomach to disappoint them...must keep my thoughts and feelings for Gio to myself and go through with this charade marriage to Marco.

"I'm fine, Mama. It's only nerves. There are so many people coming, and I will be the center of attention. It's making me anxious, that's all. I'll be fine once I arrive at the church and the festivities begin."

Studying my daughter's face...don't totally believe her...I'm afraid to push for answers. I've been praying Andrea would forget Giu...afraid if I broach that subject, I might not be able to live with my daughter's reply. I only hope I won't live to regret my reluctance to contradict my husband's wishes on the forbidden subject of Gio Daleo. My mother-in-law, Angela's death bed words are echoing in my head. "Remember Maria, protect your daughter from the rules of others. Let her find her own love and her own life."

With denial and wishful thinking, Maria blocked the words that drifted through her memories.

Anyway, it seems... Andrea has recovered from her

malaise...just suspicion...nothing is awry...it's only wedding jitters.

Giving Andrea a loving hug, she motioned her to the stairs to get going.

"So, let's get moving, my dear. Today is to be the best day of your life."

Maria secured the endless row of satin buttons running up the back of Andrea's gown. Maria and their close family friend, Ella, had taken weeks to make Andrea's gown. Ella's creations were always the talk of the town, and as a team, they created an angel's dress. It was heavenly. A small gather off the shoulders revealed Andrea's swan-like neck, and a pinched pearl sequence circled her tiny waist. A satin train, almost ten feet long, flowed like a billowy, white cloud.

An afternoon breeze blew in through the open bedroom window and brought a sticky balm to the already stuffy air. During the quiet moments alone with her mother, Andrea rethought her dilemma. Tempted to share her true feelings, she started to speak a few times, but stopped. She just couldn't get the words out. Ultimately, she remained silent and grew increasingly claustrophobic.

These walls are closing in on me...I can't get enough air.

As Maria placed the delicate crown topping the virgin veil upon Andrea's flowing dark waves, she stepped back to admire the gossamer vision of her beautiful daughter.

Not able to take another minute of her mother's fussing and feigning a case of nerves to cover up her panic and dizziness, Andrea shoed her mother off with the pretense that Maria needed time to get ready herself.

At long last alone, and with her spirit low, Andrea sank into her bedside chair, not concerned about the wrinkles in the satin gown that billowed up around her.

Finally able to take a deep breath, Andrea sobbed, "Truly, I'm trapped. What can I do now that it's too late?" I've tried my best to hide my anguish from my parents…I have no choice…I must go through with this marriage to Marco!"

Andrea really had tried to honor her father's demand to stop seeing Giu. Fear of her father's anger had put a stop to most of their meetings down by the river, but not all of them. As innocent as their trysts had been, she knew she had no alternative but to listen to her father's demands, but she couldn't resist seeing Giu. She tried, but could not bury her feelings. She loved her parents and had been raised to respect their wishes, so believing she had no option, Andrea accepted her fate and let her life change course, so she and Marco became the best of friends, but there was always Giu.

Even though Andrea and Marco had known each other since childhood, they'd never really gotten close until that night at her eighteenth birthday party. Once Marco sang "Happy Birthday," they'd connected like old buddies, and their friendship blossomed. They had their families in common, so it was an easy match. Marco also fit in with Andrea's friends, becoming part of the pack of teenagers who danced at the church fairs and talked until the wee hours of the night.

Andrea encouraged Marco to include his friends from the agricultural school, but he never showed interested in doing so. He seemed to enjoy her crowd so much, she never pushed the issue.

The only person Marco ever introduced to the circle was a young man named Enzo. Andrea was so happy to have Enzo join their group of friends. She was pleased Marco at least brought one friend around with him, besides she really liked

Enzo. He was a lot like Marco, plus it was nice to see these two guys banter back and forth, adding to the group's dynamics. She learned Marco and Enzo had gone to agricultural school together and had been classmates for years. They told the story of the trip they took to Altamura and the kitchen girl, Rose, who had entertained the boys on their first trip outside their village. Each time, they'd embellish the tale with more detail to entertain her friends. It all sounded so risqué; everyone loved hearing it repeatedly.

Moreover, Andrea's girlfriends loved Marco. He laughed at their silliness and was the shoulder they found to confide their troubles. Once Marco proposed to Andrea, nothing changed. Even though they were engaged, Marco and Andrea still went out with the group, and spent their nights partying with their friends.

Andrea never had a real boyfriend, so she wasn't quite sure what to expect from Marco. Giu had kissed her and held her in his arms, but they'd never had chance to develop a real relationship, hiding away in her little cove by the river.

It had been a fun-filled night of laughter with Marco entertaining their friends with his usual repertoire of songs. At the evening's end, never expecting Andrea to make her way home alone, Marco escorted her through the darkened streets. Andrea felt giddy from the bottle of wine they'd been sipping as they partied behind the church, and her pretty dance shoes were no match for the cobbled street.

"Ouch," she cried out as she bent to grab her ankle.

Mario reached for her to keep her from falling, but she ended up in his arms. The surge of pain subsiding, she was closer to him in a way she'd never been before. Feeling a rush, she turned her head to kiss him. Her warm lips found his, but his lips didn't respond. Marco stiffened up and backed away, staring at Andrea.

An icy chill ran up Andrea's spine. The warm breeze disappeared, and the rays of moonlight fell behind the night clouds. The moment and the buzz from the wine were gone.

All the nights he never attempted to kiss me, and now he froze at the perfect chance. Are his eyes sad or embarrassed, or both? Look at him... turning away from me...not able to look at me. It's not just the kiss that's wrong...we're wrong. As husband and wife, we are going to be all wrong.

Marco witnessed everything in Andrea's face. She didn't need to say a word.

"Andrea, I...I'm sorry, so sorry. You know I love you. You know that. We have such fun together. You're my best friend. We can have a wonderful life together. Please, things will change. I promise you with all my heart."

Andrea heard Marco's pleadings drift through the night air. Saddened and rejected, she stood immobile in the street. She couldn't hate him, because she still loved her dear friend, but her platonic feelings for him weren't going to change the truth.

My heart hurts for him...his plea...so sincere...the pain in his eyes...so palpable. Spinning...what do I know about love...except the warmth I feel each time I think of Giu...always Giu. I long to see him...laugh with him...to be wrapped in his strong arms. Giu's lips are the lips I should be kissing tonight...hopeless situation...can never pursue. All these months...wished to bring up the forbidden subject of Giu with my father...haven't had the courage to disobey him...resigned myself to his decision...now set in stone by both his strengths and my weaknesses...accepted my fate.

Murmuring under her breath, Andrea confirmed her situation. "Fear of my father's wrath and my girlish insecurities have kept me from following my heart...here I am with the man my father decided was best."

As the soft glow of the moon reappeared, she turned to hearing Marco's plea.

"Andrea, please come here."

Turning back toward him, she was taken off guard when he pulled her face to his. In one quick motion, he held her against him pressing his lips down on hers.

Totally bewildered, Andrea was speechless.

Marco is two years older than me...maybe he knows more about these things...maybe things will change between us...maybe my father was right to bring us together... maybe we can have a wonderful life together.

Maybe, maybe, maybe. Without another word, Andrea took Marco's hand, and together they walked home along the winding path into the dark night.

Chapter 19
Lessons Learned
L'uomo deve trovare la propria verità
(Man must find his own truth)

What Giu never learned from his father, Ernesto, he learned from Tino. He never shook the feeling that he'd been abandoned when his father left his family when he was only ten years old. He remembered some good times before that fateful day, but not too many. The years had passed, and the good memories had faded along with the years. All he'd been left with was his anger directed against the Fioranos.

After that fortuitous morning coffee with Tino, Giu had moved with his satchel into Tino's two-bedroom flat. Having gone from growing up in a rickety house on the edge of a cliff to living on the streets, this was a safe haven and paradise to Giu.

They each had their own bedroom with beds with frames and soft mattresses. Tino's room was larger than Giu's, since it had been his bedroom with his long-gone wife, but Giu had no complaints and couldn't have been happier. His corner room off the kitchen had a window that opened to a tiny garden below and in the morning when they'd return from fishing, he'd sleep under the sash while the early breeze lulled him to sleep. Evenings, they'd make their way to the docks to get Andiamo ready to push off. They'd test the lines and examine the nets, all the while praying they'd have a good catch that night. The other fishermen were pretty much transient, coming and going month by month, except Giu. He was at the dock each evening reliable, dedicated and ready to work.

As they became trusted friends, Tino told Giu stories about his difficult youth.

"I never met my father, and my mother, the saint that she was, never recovered from losing the man she loved. So, I grew up mostly on my own, furious with the world for having to do so."

Tino's tales stirred up strong emotions in Giu. Giu tried to recall happy memories but mostly they had disappeared with time. He had no trouble remembering the years of Ernesto's drinking, the family's poverty, the shack they called a home and his mother's tears. Over time, he shared some of his past with Tino. Eventually he related the events with the Fioranos and how much he hated them for destroying his father.

Sitting quietly at a corner table at the street cafe, Tino studied Giu and finally realized the source of Giu's strife.

"You know, Giu, I listened to your story carefully this morning. Could there be any chance that the Fioranos didn't cause your father's downfall? Could he have been his own worst enemy?"

Giu's face darkened as he jumped up from the table. The chair screeched as he pushed it back.

"Tino, what do you know about my family? How can you judge my father? He was a good man who was pushed to the edge!"

Without raising his voice, Tino replied softly.

"Because Giu, I was just like him. Please sit back down and let me tell you a story."

Reluctantly, Giu pulled his chair back in and sat with one foot turned out ready to go again.

"You know I'm divorced, but I never told you the rest of the story. When I was young, I was married to the love of my life, my Bella. Shortly after we married, she got pregnant, and we were thrilled anticipating our baby's birth. In those days, I was just common laborer digging ditches for the new roads being constructed near Naples. It was dirty work, but I was young and strong, and we were happy. The money was enough to keep us going. The other road workers teased me endlessly about running home to the little lady every night after work. Many of them had been married for years and preferred to stay out at the bars instead of going home to crying children and tired women.

"So, one day after grueling hours in the sun, I gave in to their teasing and joined them. The bar was dark and cozy, and the liquor was strong and flowing. Hours later, after many a tall yarn and way too many tall drinks, I swayed out of the bar and headed home. The night air sobered me up a bit, but not like the scene waiting for me. As I climbed the stairs to our tiny apartment, I eyed the door was ajar. Bile rising in my throat, I jumped the last three steps and barreled through the door."

Tino stopped and took a deep breath. His eyes darkened and his mouth tightened.

"What I saw I can only tell you changed me. My wife lay sprawled on her back on the floor, her eyes still and wide open. Blood had seeped through her dress and was puddled around her legs."

"I'm so sorry," Giu blurted.

"No, please, let me tell you the rest. Someone had broken in. I will never know why, because we had nothing to steal, so I can only still imagine. The details, the police weren't sure, but they determined she fought back hit her head and took a hard fall. The head injury killed her, and the fall killed our unborn child."

Taking in another deep breath, he slowly blew it back out, looking into the distance as if there was an answer there waiting for him.

"After that night, I found solace in only one thing, and that was the bottle. I lost my job and took many more, but I couldn't keep a position for more than a week or two. Eventually, I'd show up drunk and fall asleep on the job. I was angry with my work buddies, because they had enticed me to have a night of drinks, but truly I was angry with myself and could not forgive myself for that one night that changed my world.

This went on for longer than I want to admit, until one day I wandered into a church in Naples. It was eerily quiet and smelled like burning brush. I hadn't been in a church in years, and I don't know what bought me there. I'd like to think it was my loving wife from heaven directing me to my forgiveness. Out of nowhere, I felt frightened. I had an overwhelming need to run. I knew if I stayed I'd have to face the truth, and I was afraid to open old wounds. But I stayed. It was as if a hand touched my shoulder and guided me to a pew. I knelt in front of that alter and cried like a baby. Time passed until I was finally spent. Hearing footsteps, I turned to see a priest solemnly looking at me.

'My son, I've been in the back of the church for a while, however I didn't want to interrupt your time alone with God. You know, sometimes we find ourselves in places not knowing how we got there. Life can be mysterious that way.'

"I remember thinking, what a strange thing to say, but at the same time knowing exactly what he meant. The old padre and I sat in that pew, until I had nothing left inside to share. I left the church cleansed that day. I felt freer than I had in years. Somehow with the grace of God, I'd found a path to forgiving myself."

Giu stared at Tino, trying to digest the meaning of Tino's story.

"Tino, I truly am so sorry for your loss, but what does this have to do with my father?"

"Don't you see, Giu? We all go to dark places in our lives and some of us hurt the ones we love by chance, or by accident. Your father had his own cross to bear, and he couldn't deal with it. You relay your mother's history with your father. No one ever knew your father's past, or for that matter where he came from. When he first fell in love with your mother, maybe he buried his troubles for a while, but they just wouldn't stay buried. He turned to drink to heal his wounds, but all that did was make things worse. Did you ever think that he hated himself for what he was doing to your mother and your family? Your father couldn't stop drinking, and he couldn't forgive himself, so he left. Did you ever think that maybe the Fioranos, who you hate so much, were not the cause of his problems? Do you think maybe it's time to forgive your father and to allow yourself a life absent of this bitterness?"

It was a great deal for Giu to absorb. He'd never thought of his life from a different point of view before. Tino's words reached a place deep inside, and the urge to fight back or run disappeared. With a tired smile, he nodded his head.

"You've given me a lot to think about, Tino, my friend. Let's go home and get some sleep. Remember we have work to do tonight"

After that night in the church, Tino came to grips with his past and was finally able to move on with his life without carrying the burden of anger and fear. He'd found his way, bought Andiamo, and made a good living. Now, content and feeling fated to meet Giu, he hoped he could help Giu also find a new direction. So, they became boss and crewman, but much more than that in a very short time. Tino took Giu under his wing and taught him everything he knew about boats and fishing and the truths in life.

Alici fishing is successful when the seas are calm. Andiamo started out just before dark to make it to the best fishing spot about an hour or so directly out to sea. The weather was typical, and there was nothing different or special about the night. Once the boat reached the school, which was shoaling as it should, the men dropped the nets and scooped the fish into the boat, a routine like any other night.

But, that night was far from an ordinary night. An unexpected wind struck up, and the air quickly chilled. Before anyone realized it, black clouds blocked the moon's light and fast wind blew the oil lanterns out. An unexpected storm was brewing, as the blackish waters began to churn. Tino barked orders to his men, and everyone scurried to obey. The men had seen squalls before and knew this kind of storm was nothing to ignore.

Giu had been fishing with Tino for many seasons, and had seen some bad weather, but he'd never experienced the wrath of the sea. When Tino first sensed the impending storm, he'd strapped Giu to the helm, hoping the stabilization would aid Giu's strong arms in holding the wheel.

First a roar, then an unpredictable avalanche of death,

smashed into the port side and propelled the boat and the crew into the air. With all of Tino's might and Giu's strength, toII-gether they couldn't wrench the wheel to turn the boat back into the rogue wave.

There was no up, no down, then it all crashed into a dull silence.

The violet sky was calm, and the world now stood still, as dawn approached from the East. The only sound, a seagull's cry, woke Giu from his daze. Alone, bloodied and worn, Giu was still strapped to the helm.

Tino was gone. His body-never found after that dreadful stormy night. Dehydrated and sunburned, but fortuitously teth-ered to the wheel, Giu was saved by a passing fishing boat and returned to shore. There wasn't much left of Andiamo, and there was no sign of the rest of the crew.

After a month in a public infirmary, Giu returned to the only home he knew, Tino's apartment. Opening the door to silence for the first time since the accident, he broke down sob-bing. His friend was gone, and he was alone in the world again. He collapsed on his bed and starred at the ceiling until morn-ing.

It's strange how weeks turn into months and months turn into years. Life goes quickly that way. We think we have forever, then before we know it, time is gone. When I left home, I had no idea where I was going or for how long. It's been almost three years since I left my mother, Francesco and Isabella. So much has happened in this short time. Most im-portantly, my time with Tino changed my life. Tino taught me how to be a man, to face up to my pain and make peace with it. It took all of this heartache to finally realized I've been blessed with only one life, and that it's up to me to make the most of it. It took me a while, but after our talk that day at the cafe, Tino's words sunk in, and slowly I began to forgive my father for his sins. I finally realized my father's demons had nothing to do with me. I also forgave my mother. All those years, I could hear her say, "You're nothing but a drunk. Get out of here and never come back!" Now, through the eyes of a man, no longer a child, I stopped blaming her for those words.

With the dawn, he shuffled to the kitchen. Aching and still recovering, he staggered from weeks of inactivity. The coffee was hot, but Giu couldn't warm up. After sitting for a while in a daze just staring at the wall, he realized he needed to try to find someone, anyone, related to Tino. He had to tell them Tino was dead.

Coffee cooling in hand, he slowly walked into Tino's bedroom remembering Tino kept a small, metal box on the old, wooden dresser next to his bed. Embarrassed to be going through his friend's things, he opened the latch in hopes something would direct him. Most were trinkets, memories that Giu would have no way of understanding, a few letters, but no addresses, only scripted signatures of a time long past. Giu lifted out the last stash of life's reminders, but nothing was there to give him an inkling of a relative. Then, he saw his name boldly scripted across an envelope, *FOR GIO.*

A chill came over him. Slowly, hands now shaking, he slid the envelope open to read his friend's message from the grave.

My dear friend, Giu,
If you are reading this letter, I must be gone. I'm not sure what got me, the sea or some woman I slighted, but gone.
You came into my life and became the son I never had.

From the moment we met, I saw myself in you. Your tough hide, strong work ethic, and your hard head-it was like looking at my younger self in a mirror. I've been blessed to have you in my life, for however long that's been.

I believe in my heart you've grown and fought your adversities and can have a life, a real life of your own choosing.

You'll find a lock box under my bed. The key is at the bottom of the coffee can in the kitchen cupboard.

In it is the deed to this apartment and the deed and insurance for Andiamo. There's money in the box, too. I've been saving for years and haven't had any reason to spend any of it.

There's no one to find. I don't have any living relatives, and do yourself a favor, my dear boy, don't go looking for my ex-wife!

Giu, it's all yours. I want you to sell what you can and take everything and go find your family. See your mother, hug her and tell her you're okay. She deserves the peace of knowing you're alive. Laugh with your brother and sister. Try to remember the good times together. Forget the bad. Don't carry it with you. It's poison, and you have the choice to leave it behind.

Enjoy your life, and remember I loved you like a son.
Your dear friend,
Tino

Tears streamed down Giu's face as he sank on to Tino's old mattress. Sobbing in disbelief, he didn't try to wipe the tears away. Tino's last words echoed throughout the room touching his heart and soul. Tino had saved him in so many ways, and now Giu owed it to Tino to live the life he'd been given.

Chapter 20
The Plea and the Promise
La verità ci conduce al nostro destino
(The truth leads us to our destiny)

Andrea struggled, knowing her marriage to Marco was only hours away.

After the night Marco pulled away from her kiss, she tried to believe things would work out between them. They both acted as if the night never happened, as though nothing was wrong. Pretending, they went about living their lives, but she was very clear she was on a devastating path with nowhere to turn off.

Now, sitting in a wrinkled wedding gown with no desire to finish getting ready, Andrea recalled that dreadful day at the cheese factory when she found out the truth about Marco, and sadly did nothing about it.

Marco's friend, Enzo, worked for Marco's family in their cheese business. He'd graduated from agricultural school with Marco, so he was a perfect hire for floor work, but there wasn't an open position. Marco managed to persuade his father to hire Enzo anyway as an extra floor supervisor. So, Marco and Enzo best friends from their school years, remained tight and worked together every day.

Andrea seldom went to the cheese factory. She usually met Marco after he finished work. Nights, he'd come by her house and talk about their family cheese and wine businesses with her father and compliment her mother's cooking. Once the niceties were over, she'd sit with Marco outside, or they'd head out to the church dances with their friends.

However, on this inauspicious day, she'd come up with a great idea, but she wasn't sure Marco would agree. He had such a beautiful voice, so she thought it would be wonderful if he sang a sweet song, like a *serenata,* to her at the wedding reception. She couldn't contain herself until that evening to run her charming idea by him, so she set off for the factory.

It was lunchtime, so the floor workers were outside in the field near the factory buildings sitting in the shade to escape the noonday sun. She spotted Marco's father, Marino, standing in the distance holding court with his men. A few hearty laughs floated through the air as she walked through the building portico.

The floors were wet from the water used to spray the floors clean each day before lunch. Netting was tied to the sides of huge, copper vats holding balloons of cheese in place until the men returned from their long break. Everything was silent. In order not to slide on the slippery floors, Andrea tip toed through the sterile hall to Marco's office. She reached the door, but before she turned the doorknob, a strange moan came from inside the office. A small window next to the door was covered with heavy, wooden blinds which blocked the sightline into the room, but one slat was broken giving Andrea a clear view.

Marco and Enzo.

Startled in disbelief, she looked straight through the broken slat again. Her eyes hadn't lied. Distraught and not wanting to be discovered, she quietly turned and slid away past the cheese vats through the portico to the fresh air. Marino was still talking with the workers, and no one took notice of her. Once out of their sight, she ran and ran. Crying as she stumbled down the hill, she raced to her solitary spot along the river. It was now just before one o'clock, and the sun was still bright in the sky. Andrea tucked herself into the cove to get out of the hot rays. Finally, she let her sobs out. No one would hear her this far from the village.

How could I have been so stupid? Did I miss every clue? Enzo was the only friend...Marco's lack of desire for me...promised things would change. Our engagement came out of nowhere...just good friends...the olive grove story...Rose the kitchen girl. Marco and Enzo always exchanged a look...thought they didn't want to admit...the entertainment with Rose...that was never the case.

Andrea sat for a long time. The sun moved higher in the sky behind the ridge of her hidden cove. Afternoon was almost early evening, and when she finally looked up, a black cloud was moving across the sky hanging low over the entrance to her cave. Familiar with the late afternoon storms, she jumped up to rush home before the skies opened. She darted up the hill and just as she got to the top, a bang of thunder clapped over her head, and then in seconds a flash of lightning hit the tree closest to her. She had nowhere to run but back to the cove. Soaked from the heavy rain, she ran back down the hill to her hide-a-way.

Drying off as she waited out the storm, she prayed for

guidance.

I have to do something about this wedding...what to do....I can never tell Marco what I saw...I love Marco like a brother...I can never let his secret be known...it will destroy his life and his family. I need to get out of this marriage without anyone ever knowing why. I want to go to Giu...tried to stay away from him out of fear and respect for my father...haven't succeeded...cried on Giu's shoulder so many times over these past months. We've fallen in love...can't bear to be away from him, let alone marry a man I love only like a brother. I thought things couldn't get any worse...until today...Marco and Enzo in the darkened office...dear lord.

Once the sky cleared, partially dry, but shivering, Andrea headed back up the hill. She had to confide in someone. She had to see Giu.

Andrea and Giu had a secret code. If Andrea could sneak away and meet Giu after Sunday mass, she'd tie a pink ribbon on the cemetery gate. The ribbons were so tiny, no one paid any attention to the ones she'd tied so far. So, on her way back home, she detoured to the cemetery and tied another ribbon knowing her signal would alert Giu to meet her at their cove on Sunday morning.

Sunday morning came, and Giu faithfully waited as anticipated. Tearfully, Andrea shared what she saw in the cheese factory office. Giu begged her to tell Marco she knew about his secret.

"Andrea, my love, it's the only way out of this marriage. Marco will be forced to break off the engagement and that will leave you free to be with me."

"Oh, Giu, that's not the case. I know I won't be quite free. I totally understand the history between our families. That puts you in a bad light with my father. Besides, your delinquent behavior growing up, and the fact that you went off for years leaving your mother and siblings to fend for themselves, will not put you in any better favor. I know there's nothing I can do to change my miserable path. We both know my father will never bless our union."

Vincenzo and Maria, dressed in their finest, waited in the kitchen anticipating their daughter's entrance.

Still sitting motionless, Andrea grew more despondent.

My wedding,...just an hour away...time ticking,..minutes flying. Here I am in my wedding gown getting dressed for a wedding to the wrong man.

Andrea reached for the traditional Italian wedding garter. Preoccupied, she pulled it up over her ankle and up her calf until it sat heavily on her thigh. Sighing, and almost in tears, she put her head against the back of the chair.

What will tonight be like? I'll be sharing a bed with Marco, not Giu. I'll live a loveless life, sad and alone.

Knowing she could no longer prolong the inevitable, she emerged from her bedroom to find her parents waiting. Vincenzo was beaming, and Maria looked beautiful in a soft rose-colored dress covered in tiny, white pearls that she'd made for the occasion. Faking a smile, Andrea held each of their hands and together they walked out of the house to make their way to Saint Matthew's Church.

When they reached the church steps, all was still quiet. Everything had been arranged to perfection earlier in the day, and the guests were not expected for more than an hour. To respect the village tradition, Vincenzo and Maria left Andrea at the church door. It was now her time to enter the church alone to pray for God's blessings on her marriage. They hugged and held her in their arms for a long moment, turned down the steps and made their way to the little annex to await the wedding hour.

Andrea entered the silent vestibule. Her footsteps echoed in the hushed air. White roses and lilies filled the glorious alter and tiny lily of the valley bouquets wrapped in pink ribbon tied the entrance to each pew. It was breathtaking, and her heart suffered more. Finally, reaching the altar, she knelt to begin her prayers, but she couldn't bring herself to pray for marriage blessings. All she could think of was a prayer to Mary to help with her suffering. Silent at first and then, barely audible, she recited from memory:

> *Mary, protector of all women;*
> *Champion of the most desperate;*
> *Mother most divine, most loving;*
> *I pray to you today.*
> *Consider my anguish and my heartache*

Choaking up and not able to go on, tears streamed down her cheeks as she sobbed and clutched her hands to her breast.

Whispering through tears, she cried, "Dear God, what am I to do?"

Father Falchi hummed to himself as he arranged the vestments for the upcoming ceremony. What a glorious day for faith and love and hope. The sacristy followed behind the altar with two entrances into the church, and the West door to the gospel side was open for his upcoming entrance. Hearing a muffled cry, he stopped humming and moved toward the door. There was the young bride, Andrea Fiorano, breath stuttering as she gasped for air. Not to startle her, Father Falchi cautiously walked across the altar. Andrea, seeing him getting closer, wiped her swollen eyes and kept her head bowed.

"My dear child, are you all right? Today is your wedding

day, a beautiful day for celebration, not tears."

As he came closer, Andrea finally looked at him through her blurred vision.

Oh, my dear Mary. I prayed, and this is my prayer answered. My anguish is no longer a secret. I finally have the strength I've been searching for.

Andrea slowly rose to stand.

"Father, this is not a day for celebration. This is a day of deceit. My marriage to Marco is a deception on his part and on mine. To marry us would be a travesty."

With many years as the spiritual leader for his parish Catholics, Father Falchi had seen a lot in his tenure, but this was a first.

Before he could speak, Andrea went on, "I love Marco, but I cannot marry him. We are like brother and sister, and there is no hope for anything more. He has fooled himself into believing there can be more, that we can have love like a man and wife. I should have stopped this charade many weeks ago, but I too thought we would grow to love each other. Most of all, I didn't want to disappoint my parents who wanted this marriage from the beginning,"

Now feeling a force rise within, Andrea wiped away her tears and stood straighter.

"The truth, Father, is one day I went to Marco's cheese factory, and God forgive me, accidentally saw Marco with his friend, Enzo. They were in an embrace. No, that's not even close to the truth. It was much more than an embrace. Do you understand? Please don't make me say it."

She paused to catch her breath.

"So, you see, this marriage is a mistake. I never wanted to hurt Marco, so I could never tell anyone what I saw, let alone him. Please give me your word that you will never repeat a word of this to anyone-ever."

The priest was stunned. He stood motionless, except for his head nodding acceptance. He was now forever bound to keep this secret to appease Andrea's pleading tears.

"I prayed to the Virgin Mary today, and you were the answer to my prayers. Now, please let me leave out the side door. Please, Father, don't try to stop me."

Before he could open his mouth, Andrea gathered the train of her gown in one hand and brushed past him as she hurried out the side door.

After Andrea's outburst, Father stood motionless in the still church air for what seemed an eternity. There was so much to process, but most of all, his oath to secrecy.

Unbeknownst to both Andrea and Father Falchi, as Andrea rushed out the side door, there was a soft, scurrying step and a shadow quickly made its way past the open east-side sacristy door.

Andrea fled down the hill behind the church tripping over her gown, ripping the hem as she escaped. With each panicked step, her tears poured, until she found herself at the hill by her favorite spot near the river.

Nestled back in the cove Giu sat loitering, resigned that the love of his life was marrying Marco.

I can't stop this wedding. This will be my last visit here at our hidden cove...one last time to soothe my soul with memories of our secret meetings. I wish I could expose this charade, but I know in my heart I could never do that to Marco or to Andrea. This secret is theirs to tell, not mine...I could never betray them. I knew this day was coming...My heart is heavy, but I have no choice...I'm prepared to leave Sicignano deli Alburni forever.

I came home as a promise to Tino's memory. I reunited

with my mother...I let her know that I've grown to be a good man. I bonded with my siblings...tried to make up some of the lost time for all the years I've missed. After finding Tino's letter in Tino's apartment, I lived by my oath to Tino...to make something out of my life. I made good on my promise to my dead friend by returning home to my family, but I didn't expect to find my life's love. Tino told me to go home and live a good life, as if he knew that's where my life would come together.

Andrea is a breath of fresh air...so unlike the girls I've known in Naples. She is beautiful...clever and has a good heart. But, I know I have to leave my birth home...sadly I have to leave Andrea. I'll never be able to live close by watching her pass me in the winding alleys of Sicignano. I will never be able to attend Sunday mass with her sitting rows in front of me next to Marco. Living my life without her, except as a passing shadow of our love, will be torture, so I've made my decision to leave.

I've said goodbye to my family...taking care to ensure my mother has all she needs. I left her with a secure future... knowing my siblings live nearby and her grandchildren spend most days in her yard. I'm confident she will always be safe and loved.

My new river boat is packed, and I'm ready to say goodbye to the home of my youth, my family and the girl of my dreams. I will travel slowly down the river...until it reaches the coast, but from there...I'm not sure. Will I make my way back to Tino's apartment in Naples which is now mine? I've got money, but what good is it? My heart is broken, but like it or not...I have to move on.

Stalling his departure, he rested against the stone cliff just outside the cool cove where he'd met Andrea so many blissful days. He knew he should leave because the afternoon was passing, but something kept him rooted to the spot.

A ruckus of stones toppling down the hill, shook him out of his reflection. He abruptly turned to the sound. Andrea, in her disheveled wedding gown, was stumbling down the slope toward him, hair falling in her face and eyes swollen.

Giu couldn't move fast enough. He pushed himself off the crumbling wall and rushed up the slope. Andrea ran toward him with open arms.

Chapter 21
The Realization
L'Amore conquista tutto
(Love conquers all)

Outside, in the church annex, Vincenzo and Maria quietly reminisced over the wonderful moments they'd had with Andre from the time she was born. They were waiting for Andrea to complete her prayers for blessings until it was time to enter the church. What a glorious day! Their little girl was marrying the son of their good friend.

As they climbed the worn, stone steps, a grey cloud blew across the sky. Maria hoped there wasn't a storm brewing. Rain would ruin the outdoor celebration planned for that evening. They entered the church expecting to see Andrea finishing her prayers, but she wasn't there. They stood at the back of the church, confused.

Vincenzo reacted first.

"Where is she? Maria, there is no one in the church."

A commotion was coming for the sacristy. Turning to Maria, Vincenzo asked, "Is that Marco?"

Moments before, when Andrea had confided in Father Falchi, Enzo, Marco's friend, had come into the sacristy to check the wedding preparations. His heart was broken knowing Marco was to marry Andrea, but there was no choice. It was best. He loved Marco, but there would never be a future for them, so with a saddened heart, he'd given his blessings, until today. He knew now that Andrea knew the truth. He overheard her pledge Father Falchi to secrecy. He saw her run.

Ready for his wedding day, Marco entered the church from the West side and found Enzo checking the altar preparations. Enzo was flushed and anxious. He grabbed Marco by the shoulders and talked so fast Marco couldn't understand what was happening.

"She's gone...she told Father...he took an oath. Please, Marco, don't follow her. Let her go."

Marco pulled Enzo aside. "What are you saying? Who's gone? What oath? Please get a hold of yourself!"

Startled into calming down, Enzo blurted out the details of what he'd witnessed.

Deflated, Marco sat heavily into the priest's velvet chair while murmuring under his breath.

"Dear God, what has happened? Poor Andrea, what have I done to her? How could I let it get this far? My family will never forgive me. Oh, my God, everyone will know."

Marco sat silent and stunned. Enzo, a few feet behind him, stood still in shock.

Just then, Father Falchi entered the sacristy. Marco's heart stopped.

"My dear young man, I have something devastating to tell you. Your future wife, Andrea, was here today praying for her marriage blessings, when she heard a voice. The voice told her she had a higher calling and could not marry you. I came on the scene just as she was leaving, and she told me what had occurred. So, you see my boy, she is gone, and this wedding will not be."

The priest hoped to God he'd be forgiven for this lie. With no time to think, he'd come up with the best story he could to keep his vow of silence to Andrea.

Enzo was grateful, but overwhelmed that the truth was out.

Can this man of God have a heart this grand? He knows the facts, but to his oath, he stands in this church telling a false story to save us both.

Panicking, he turned away and bolted from the sacristy.

Marco, now alone with the priest, tried to gather his thoughts, but before he could speak, Andrea's parents broke into the room.

"Where is our daughter? What is happening here? Marco where is Andrea?"

Marco was so shaken, he sat immobile, blankly starring at the Fioranos.

Recognizing Marco was speechless, Father Falchi carefully stepped up taking each of their hands in his.

"My dear friends, there has been a terrible upset. Andrea left the church saying she could not marry today, that she'd heard a voice telling her she had a higher calling. I couldn't stop her. Marco just entered and has just now heard the same news. I am so sorry for your heart break. I will leave you now with your thoughts to give you time to talk and to pray."

"What are you talking about, Father?" Vincenzo was in a panic. Nothing was making sense.

Stumbling, Maria found her way to a worn pew collapsing onto the hard, wood seat.

Dear God, I should have known better. This marriage was not right for my daughter. She's been in love with Giu all this time... I knew it in my heart. It is my fault. I was afraid...to counter my husband's wishes...to know the truth. I've betrayed my daughter. Please, dear Lord...please forgive me.

Vincenzo's temper was rising, and he was quickly losing control. He grabbed at the priest's arm to force him to turn around to face him.

Calmly Father Falchi turned to Vincenzo, but before he could respond, Maria, realizing she had to put a stop to her husband's fury before things went too far, interceded.

"Vincenzo, please stop. Neither Father Falchi nor Marco have any wrong in this. The blame is with you and with me. This is not the time or place to air our sorrows. Stretching across the void to an infuriated Vincenzo, she pleaded, "Please take my hand and leave with me now."

Hearing the strength in his wife's voice and recognizing her resolve, Vincenzo apologized to the priest and quickly moved with his wife toward the exit door. They needed to sort everything out, but even in his rage, he realized this was not the place to do it.

Father Falchi exhausted from the turmoil, turned to leave. He gave a slight nod of the head to Macro, a sign his secret would forever be kept.

Down at the river's edge, Andrea couldn't believe her fate. Astonished at his good luck, Giu took her in his arms and held her against his heart until she stopped shaking. The heat of the day was waning as the sun laid low in the sky. Grasping the urgency of the situation and knowing time was not on their side, Giu asked Andrea if she would be willing to leave her home and her family and forge a new life with him.

"Andrea, I need you to listen carefully. I promise I will care for you forever and build a wonderful life for us if you will come with me and start anew. But I need you to understand the depth of this decision. You will be leaving your home and your family. It won't be easy."

Leaving a burnt path and knowing there was no going back, Andrea replied.

"I do understand, Gio, and my answer is a clear yes, yes a thousand times."

She was with the man she loved, and her heart was telling her the way. By running from her wedding to Marco, she'd finally found her strength.

Slowly, the boat pushed offshore. The last site Andrea ever saw of her home was Castello di Giusso crowning the hilltops of her precious village. The sun set golden, dropping behind them, as the boat moved west into the dark of the night.

Chapter 22
The Journey
La vita è un sogno
(Life is a dream)

Luckily, Giu had been prepared for a journey, be it alone. He'd packed the boat with blankets, along with food and water, so he knew they were safe on the river and had enough provisions for several days.

Exhausted from the day, Andrea slept peacefully against his arm as if she didn't have a care in the world. And, now with Andrea snuggled at his side while he maneuvered the river toward the sea, Giu finally felt a peace in his heart that had evaded him his whole life.

But the stillness in his heart did not still his worried mind. Not wanting to upset an already distraught girl, Giu kept his thoughts to himself.

Truly, what am I going to do? My destination hadn't mattered to me, but now I have Andrea to care for... I must be clear on how to accomplish that.

Drifting into the night, blanketed by the sparkling stars above, Giu recalled a conversation he'd had with Tino a long while ago. Tino told him that if he'd been a younger man, he'd have found a way to go to America. He called it the "new world", a place to start over and live a new life. Tino's words hit Giu like a bolt of lightning. He'd been searching his soul for direction, and here were Tino's words coming from the heavens to guide him again. Giu knew what he needed to do. When Andrea woke, Giu had already docked the boat and arranged for travel to Naples. He would return with Andrea to Tino's apartment until he could secure steerage on a steamship. Together, he and Andea would start fresh on the other side of the world.

First, he needed to do the right thing. There was no way he could bring her into his home without her becoming his wife. So, when they arrived in Naples, after getting Andrea settled into the apartment, he went shopping for the things he thought she would need. He returned with a basket of gifts, including a dress he hoped would fit along with a strand of coral beads, and an ebony hair comb similar to the one she'd left behind.

Having lived in Naples for enough years to know a few connected people, Giu called on an old friend of Tino's from the local church. He couldn't tell him the whole story, but said he'd fallen in love and needed to do the right thing by his girl. He asked if he could he speak with the priest to arrange a quick marriage at the church of Saint Mary. All of Tino's friends missed him and also knew Giu had become like a son to him, so getting the occasion arranged wasn't difficult.

Fresh and beautiful, Andrea appeared on the threshold of the apartment balcony, taking Giu's breath away. She'd curled her hair and secured it into a bun with the new comb leaving tendrils brushing her neck. Beaming, she spun around for him to see. She'd dressed in the pale, pink dress with soft ruffled sleeves that capped her delicate wrists just above her graceful fingers. The coral beads circled her neck and dropped low on her bosom. Giu knelt on one knee on that balcony on that fortuitous day and could hardly ask his question before Andrea responded, "Yes, my love. Yes, I will...for forever and a day."

In her pale pink dress and coral beads, Andrea married her Giu. It wasn't the wedding she'd always fantasized about with a hundred guests and violins, but it was the wedding of her dreams to the man she loved.

Once married, Giu put thoughts of his hillside hometown and everything that happened there behind him. Maybe he hadn't done the right thing by the Fiorano family by stealing Andrea away down the river, but he'd done the right thing by marrying her and pledging to respect and love her forever.

Andrea, on the other hand, was in love, but distraught. Naples was a big city compared to Sicignano, and she knew no one. They were living in Giu's apartment by the thriving port of Naples, Porto Di Napoli, one of the busiest ports in all of Italy. From the small balcony, she could see the expansive half-moon bay curve out from the shore. The panorama of the breathtaking ocean seemed to go on forever. Rows of roof tops and multicolored apartments stacked up around her blanketing the dramatic faces of the cliffs.

Mornings, when Giu went off to get their affairs in order, she'd stare out on the endless blue trying to imagine America and what their life would look like there. But her longing for their future wouldn't separate from her pining for her family back home.

My parents must think I am dead. How could I leave them in the church and elope with another man, especially Giu

*Daleo...the one man my father forbade me to see? I love Giu
and can't imagine living without him, but what can I do to make
things right and ease my pain? I worry my guilt will eventually
ruin my life and my marriage.*

Giu was busy each day preparing for their steamship
voyage across the great Atlantic. There was so much for him to
do and much for him to worry about. Once their tickets were
procured, he asked a local magistrate, another old friend of
Tino's, to meet at the corner bar.

"Lorenzo, we're leaving for America soon with no contacts in the new world. As you know, I'm a fisherman by trade
and have the physical stamina and strength to put in a good
day's work. But I don't know anyone there. Tino told me stories of your trips to New York, so I thought you might be able
to assist me in connecting with a job."

Strong and broad shouldered, Lorenzo slapped Giu on
the back almost knocking him and his beer over.

"My boy, do I have contacts for you! I have family in
upstate New York. They are from Naples and own a market in
Seneca, New York. They sell meats and fish. You would be a
perfect fit."

Giu couldn't believe his good luck. He had scratched his
head for days, trying to figure out how to set their future, and
Lorenzo had fixed his worries in one quick slap.

"Jesus, Lorenzo, you'd do that for me?"

"Absolutely, my friend, for you and for Tino, and for
that cutie I see you holding and walking in the moonlight. Everyone deserves a chance, and you, my boy, have paid your
dues."

Andrea couldn't sit still another minute. The thought of going off into the busy, city streets without Giu made her anxious, but she decided to go for a walk anyway to take her mind off her worries. Wrapped in a soft, coral shawl to brave the chill, she stepped out onto the bustling street. The market stands were only a few blocks away where she knew she could get some fresh mozzarella and a bunch of flowers for the kitchen table.

Darting in and out of carts and sidestepping potholes in the dirt, Andrea made her way to the cheese stand tucked among the other rickety farm stalls along the bay. She'd come here with Giu and remembered this farmer sold the best cheese of all the peddlers. Wrapped goods in hand, she wandered through the maze, trying to remember the side street for the flower shop. Confused, she turned down a lane, straying from the life and frenzy of the market stalls. Already uneasy about leaving the apartment, the wrong turn and the isolation of the neighborhood shook her. The dimly lit backstreet lacked all the vibrance of the port. Air- drying clothes hanging above her head blocked out the daylight. Music drifted from an open window, off-pitch like a child practicing the violin. An abandoned butcher shop's door was nailed shut, and a sign hanging in the window announced it was permanently closed. Panicking, she turned to retrace her steps back to the port. Just then the door next to the butcher shop opened. Before she could see who was coming out, she heard a laugh and a familiar voice.

"Gino, I'll be back in an hour. I'm going to get the best booze for our little get together tonight. The girls will love us!"

Frozen, Andrea stood face to face with her brother, Luca.

"Jesus, Mary and Joseph. Jesus," cursed Luca. "My eyes are tricking me. This can't be. We have looked for you everywhere. Everyone thought you were dead. Andrea, are you really standing in front of me?"

From shock to tears, Andrea fell into her brother's arms, her body shaking with sobs. All the guilt she'd carried poured out in wet tears on her brother's chest. Placing his hands on her shoulders, Luca pulled her away and held her at arm's length to get a good look at his sister.

"I'm so sorry, Luca," Andrea pleaded. "Please forgive me. I could not marry Marco for two reasons. The first, I will never share. The second, I fell in love with Giu Daleo."

Not believing his ears, "You what? You know how father feels about him. How could you do this? What are you doing in Naples on this side street by yourself?"

Andrea took his hand in hers as they stood on the deserted, back street. Taking in a deep breath, she quietly told her story, leaving out Marco's secret.

"So, you see. Giu is not at fault. His boat was packed, and he had accepted my marriage to Marco and was leaving me and Sicignano forever. I ran from the church and found him just before he set off. The rest is what it is."

"Are you telling me you are living here in Naples with Giu?"

"Yes, Luca, but there is something I haven't shared. I'm married," she raised her left hand and turned it so he could see her wedding band, and with her right hand she pressed her belly, "and, I'm with child."

There was no going back. Married and pregnant, his sister had sealed her fate. Luca knew Andrea's strength and determination and knew pushing her for the reasons not to marry Marco would get him nowhere. Moreover, he never disliked Giu, as he too was a family rebel. However, he knew his parents were suffering terribly and needed to do something to ease their pain.

"Andrea, I see that fate has taken its course, and there is no turning down a different path. However, you must make amends with Father and ease Mother's torment. Come home with me and tell them your tale."

Andrea knew she would never leave a second time if she made her way back to her family and her childhood home. She also felt in her heart that her life with Giu would never be free of grief if they didn't follow their plans to leave Italy and sail to America.

"Luca, there's one more thing. We're leaving for America in two weeks. We need a fresh start for our marriage and our child, so I won't be swayed."

The shock on Luca's face told of his heart's dismay. With nothing more to say, he took her satchel of cheese and her hand.

"Let's go see Giu. It's time we talked."

Excited by his meeting with Lorenzo, Giu rushed home to share the good news with Andrea. Bursting into the apartment, he abruptly stopped and stood in the uncustomary silence. Calling out, "Andrea, Andrea," his heart started to pound. She wasn't there.

Dear God, what had happened? She'd never gone off on her own before.

Just then, he heard multiple sets of footsteps. Swinging the door open Andrea stood at the top of the landing with her brother, Luca.

Relieved to see Andrea and shocked to see Luca, Giu stood in the empty room, dumbfounded. All he could manage to say was, "Andrea ... Luca?"

The air in the room was awkward and tense, but Andrea

quickly took the lead and directed the two men to the sofa.

"Listen to me, please. Giu, you have no fault in this. I've told Luca I ran from the church on my own and found you leaving me forever. I couldn't live with marrying Marco, and I couldn't live without you. So here we are. I also told Luca we are leaving for America."

Turning her gaze toward Luca, she continued, "My heart breaks for our mother and father, and I would like to right that wrong before we leave. So, I'm asking you to arrange for us to meet here in Naples one last time. I want them to know I'm sorry for my actions, but I had no choice. I want to leave for my new life knowing we are all at peace with each other."

Both men, mouths open, made no response. They all sat quietly for a long moment, until Luca spoke.

"I can do this for you, Andrea. I take your word that Giu was not the culprit here and will share that with our father. It will break their hearts to see you go, but that will be better than believing you've come to some terrible end."

Luca had surmised she had not told Giu about the baby yet, so he said nothing. Standing slowly, he reached out for Giu's hand, "I trust my sister's life into your hands and will hold you to a promise to care and love her for as long as you shall live."

Giu's hand fitting in Luca's, replied, "Brother, I shall cherish her beyond all the days of my life."

That night after Luca left their apartment, Andra told Giu of her pregnancy. Giu held Andrea in his arms and wanted to never let go. A devoted wife, a child, and a new life in America, the stars were surely aligned.

Luca made good on his promise arranging for Andrea's new family to meet her parents and to gather one last time.

Arranging the reconciliation between his parents and Andrea and Giu was no small feat for Luca. However, once Vincenzo and Maria came to Naples, and they all stood in the small apartment together, it looked easy, as if the hand of God had interceded. Maybe it did, because what could have been a disastrous affair, surprisingly became a loving goodbye of acceptance.

Saddened, but relieved his daughter was alive and well, Vincenzo took Andrea's hand.

"Each night, look to the sky and see the moon and know I am seeing the same moon. In the morning look to the sky and know your sun is my sun. We are forever one family."

In the time Andrea had been missing, he'd done quite a bit of soul searching. With Maria's help, he'd come to realize how misguided his control had been over his daughter's life.

Looking to Giu, "I'm sorry for any ills I've caused you in the past. I was wrong to try to keep you from my daughter. It is clear to me now that love has bonds that cannot be broken. I wish you a happy life in America. May God bless you, my son."

Andrea's mother, Maria, couldn't contain her tears. Her only daughter was leaving with child to cross the ocean into a world she could only imagine. But, knowing life must take its course, she held Andrea for what felt like an eternity. Breathing in her daughter's freshly washed hair, she wished she could hold on to the scent forever. Barely able to speak, she took her daughter's face in her hands and looked into her eyes.

"Go with God, my child, and be happy. You are strong, stronger than you may think. I have faith that whatever comes your way, you will persevere. Just remember who you are and where you came from, and always follow your heart. Know I may not be going with you, but my spirit will always be by your side."

After embracing her daughter one last time, there was nothing more she could say. Tears filled her eyes, as she tried her best to smile.

Finally, at peace with her parents and their blessings, Andrea felt ready to leave Italy to find her way with her new family and a new life in America.

At that moment, if she could only envision the future, she'd see that her loving bond with her Giu would one day bring beautiful Alexandra into her life, and she'd call her granddaughter.

Part III
The Lake, Miami and Italy

Chapter 23
The Decision
Un buon amico non puo essere comprato
(A Good Friend Can't Be Bought)

Celebrating Alex's mother's 65th birthday in New York without Jake exasperated Alex.

Of course, Don Ricci had screwed everything up again. That bastard had Jake tied up on another foolish project in Miami.

August, the end of summer, bittersweet as it was, had always been family time...time for Nonna Andrea's prosciutto and fresh melon and her insalata caprese, campfires with toasted marshmallows, and goodbyes until next year. Alex's family had always adored the end of the season, soaking up the warmth of the hazy, summer days and the cool Adirondack nights.

Jake loved the D'Amato family traditions and had been looking forward to Valentina's birthday bash at the lake, but he knew he needed to appease Don Ricci by staying in Miami to finish the last-minute project Ricci had assigned. Jake needed more time before he could turn the information he compiled against Ricci and his cronies to the Securities Exchange Commission, so he didn't want any confrontations with Ricci until he contacted the SEC.

He's soothed Alex's displeasure, by promising he'd get Ricci's assignment finished as quickly as possible and fly north by the end of the week. He'd miss Valentina's 65th birthday party, so they'd just have to celebrate again when he got to Seneca.

Beautiful evening...love seeing my family all together...such characters...happy mom's night has been perfect...stars twinkling through the pine trees, reflecting on the lake water...except, no Jake...can't wait until he gets here later this week...we'll celebrate mom's birthday all over again.

Alex gathered Chris and tip-toed away from the crowd. She'd said as many 'good nights' as she could manage. The lake house was dark and eerily quiet in contrast to the festivities winding down out on the lake front. It had been a wonderful night, but Alex truly didn't enjoy herself. Something kept nudging her. She couldn't put her finger on it, something felt wrong. She tucked Chris in and made her way to the kitchen. Promising her mom she'd wait up, she filled the teapot and lit the gas stove. They'd drink sweet hot tea with milk and chitchat into the night. Waiting for the water to boil, gas flames flickered blue and yellow mesmerizing Alex.

The last song of the night drifted in...Mom's favorite, "Wishing You Love".

All things come to an end. Running through a field... frantic...searching. Where's Jake? Branches whipping my face. I see him. "Jake, stop! Don't go. Wait, I'm coming. Jake, from Boston...so sweet...embarrassing...first meeting. Who knew moguls could change a life. Please wait. Don't go there. Stop.

Wait.

First a hiss, then a sharp whistle. Alex's chin jerked up.
Jesus. I fell asleep with the gas on...crazy dream.

Black smoke filled the Miami office. Gagging, Carlo tied his
shirt tighter around his nose and mouth. Straining his back
muscles and using every bit of his arm strength, he managed to
dodge the raging fire and pull Jake by his feet around the
kitchen's center island, but then he tripped.

"What the hell?"

Collapsed across the room was another body, a body
with a singed face.

"Christ!"

Thinking quickly, knowing there was no saving this guy,
he pulled Jake's Rolex off his arm, searched his pockets for his
wallet, and pulled off his shoes. Placing Jake's belongings on
the stranger, he made the sign of the cross and pulled Jake's
badly injured body to safety.

Carlo had always been a fast thinker and always knew
when he needed to make decisive decisions. Years ago, when
he found Cara pregnant and lonely in the convent garden, he
knew right then and there that he had to save her from a lonely
life hidden away in a nunnery. This was no different. It was all
clear to him.

*Ricci's thug had tried to kill Jake and somehow the blast
killed a night worker in the kitchen. There's no way Ricci will
stop looking for Jake. He wants him dead, and he'll go to the
ends of the earth to get him. I have to make sure Ricci thinks
the job is done...pray this ploy with the watch, wallet and shoes
will work. The other guy is about Jake's height and weight... by
the time the fireman get to the building there won't be much*

left to this kitchen, let alone this guy.

There was one more thing he knew.

I have to protect Alex and Chris. If Jake survives his injuries, they can't know the truth at least until the situation is under control. Ricci threatened to harm them on the phone. I heard that, and I know Ricci will use them to get to Jake.

So, in a split second, he made his decision.

Between Two Shores   199

Chapter 24
The Plan
Cuando l'amico chiede, non v'è domani
(When a friend asks, there is no tomorrow)

Carlo's brother, Franco, lived in Italy and made a wonderful life for himself, running his hotels and his real estate investments. He was happy to stay close to where he was born and had no desire to leave as Carlo did. On the other hand, their sister, Sofia, couldn't wait to move to America. After years of begging and cajoling, she finally wore Carlo down. He sent for her, so she could enroll in college in the States. He supported her, and she did so well she was accepted at nursing school and upon graduation secured a good job at a private clinic in south Miami. Sofia idolized her brother and there was nothing she wouldn't do for him.

Carrying Jake out of the burning kitchen, especially in his compromised condition, was no easy feat, but Carlo's years of working outdoors and pure adrenalin gave him the strength to get Jake to his car. Carefully laying him across the back seat, Carlo kept thanking God that he could see Jake was still breathing.

Carlo's quick thinking put a plan in motion, and then there was no stopping it. A call to Sofia got the back door to the clinic open. Her boss did surgical procedures there, so an operating room was already set up with everything needed to stabilize Jake.

That's if they could stabilize him.

The clinic had been closed for two weeks and would remain closed due to licensing issues until all the permits were cleared. That would give Sofia a chance secretly to use whatever skills she'd perfected to keep Jake alive until Carlo could figure out what to do next. She was a registered nurse who had taken a summer training session in trauma care at Jackson Memorial Hospital. Part of that training focused on working with emergency fire victims, so that education would serve her well.

Sofia, so much like her brother, stayed calm as she sedated Jake and set intravenous lines in place to prevent dehydration. Jake was conscious, but barely breathing. He'd suffered from smoke inhalation along with heat burns from the blast. His airways were obstructed from inhaling both thermal and chemical irritants, and the trauma from the burns put him in a critical condition. Sofia did her best to administer a face mask with a high flow of oxygen, but she was concerned he needed an artificial airway to allow him to breathe, especially if his airway began to swell. She completed a careful body check to estimate the extent of trauma and tended to his burns the best she could. Finally, when she realized she couldn't do anything more, she turned to Carlo.

"I've done my best, but Jake needs a doctor. I don't want to be responsible for his death, and if I don't turn him over to a doctor, I will be accountable. He needs someone with much more experience to handle this."

How the hell am I going to get Jake the medical help he

needs and still protect him from Ricci?

"How much faith do you have in your boss? Do you think he can handle this?"

Not wanting to look at her brother, Sofia starred down at the floor. "I think he can. He's an army trained medic with a great deal of emergency experience."

"What about keeping his mouth shut? I need to know that he can keep this quiet and help me hide Jake from Ricci."

Sofia never told Carlo of her connection with her boss.

Dr. Peter Sanchez to the rest of the world, to me he's just Pete. I know my brother...he'll get all protective...I can just hear him..."Sofia, you don't know what you're doing when it comes to love." I'm not a child anymore and don't need anyone's permission. I don't have a choice. I've got to tell Carlo the truth.

Sofia lifted her head and looked her brother in the eye.

"Carlo, I know he can be trusted. We are together and have been now for almost a year. We're in love and talking about getting married. I planned to tell you, but we've been so busy here, I just didn't get around to it. He'd do anything for me, especially for you, after all you've done to support me in this country."

With everything going on, Carlo couldn't process one more thing. Normally, he'd have given a steamy, Italian big-brother reaction, just like Sofia expected, but there was no time to react or deal with this news.

Carlo just shook his head at his sister.

"There's no time for that now. Call him. Tell him you came to the clinic to get something you left behind, and found the back door jimmied. Tell him the door wasn't opened, so everything is okay, but you think he should come and take a look. When he gets here, we'll see how cooperative he chooses to be."

Within minutes the handsome doctor pushed through the clinic's back door.

"Sofia, are you ok?"

Spying Carlo, a look of complete confusion crossed his face.

"Carlo, what are you doing here? What's going on?"

Sofia reached for Pete's hand.

"I'm fine. Carlo is here because there is a situation. Please follow me."

It was evident to Carlo that Pete was crazy about his sister. He knew that look, that tender touch. It reminded him of his early days with Cara. Once Pete got past his shock and understood the urgency of the situation and the need for secrecy, Carlo was confident he had an ally in the good doctor. He felt assured Pete would do his best to save Jake, so leaving him to his work, Carlo planned the next step in saving Jake's life.

Leaving Jake in the capable hands of both his sister and her beau, Carlo sped back to Jake's office. Worried that his part in the charade would be discovered, he quickly put a story together and retraced his steps into the office parking garage. The commotion was on the upper level, fire trucks and police sirens-it was utter chaos. Rushing into the stairwell from the garage, he put his plan into action. Wanting to be seen rushing up to the sound of the commotion, he pushed open the door to the penthouse offices, sweat pouring down his face with his shirt stuck to his back. First responders were running helter-skelter crisscrossing the hall. Smoke flooded the air. The kitchen walls had collapsed, and the gas fire was still raging. He stretched his shirt up and covered his mouth to stop coughing.

A police officer hearing the choking sound, turned around just as Carlo came through the door.

"Hey, stop right where you are!"

Choking out his words, "My boss. Where's my boss? What's happened here?"

The scene started moving very fast. Carlo pulled out his ID and tried to appease the cop while he kept asking for his boss.

"Jake Reed, my boss. I was in the garage waiting for him, and I fell asleep. Then I heard all this commotion and ran up the stairs from the garage. Is he all right?"

He repeated Jake's name over and over again, hoping it would solidify in the air and help convince the police that the body he knew was lying burnt to a crisp in the kitchen was Jake Reed. The mayhem continued and Carlo didn't take the news very well. His boss was dead from an explosion. He played it up. Holding his head in his hands, Carlo slid down the wall.

"I can't believe this. What the hell happened? He just came up here to get some files. I can't believe he's dead."

Carlo went on and on acting first confused, and then angry and then defeated. Finally, a compassionate police officer took his information and escorted him out of the building. Knowing he had to keep up the sham, he headed back to Villa d'Oro dreading the call to Alex. By the time he arrived, there were police cars in the driveway. He figured they'd get there first, so he came up the rear entrance into the front hallway.

Mrs. Hermes was hysterical. She'd gotten control of herself long enough to tell the police that Alex was in New York for her mother's birthday party. She managed to give the police Valentina's phone number, so they could reach Alex. Alex was so distraught, she couldn't speak. Valentina, barely audible, tried to explain to the police that her daughter was collapsed on the stairs and couldn't come to the phone. Two officers, who'd been sent from Seneca's local precinct, were attempting to calm her down, but their efforts were of no use. Hearing the commotion through the phone, Carlo stepped up and offered to speak to Alex. Hearing Carlo was on the line, Alex took the phone.

"Oh, my God. Carlo, he's dead. Jake is dead."

"I'm so sorry, Alex. Please listen. It's going to be okay. Everything will be okay. Please try to calm down. I'm at the house trying to get more information from the police. Please take care of yourself and Chris. I'll call you at your mom's tomorrow. I'm here for you. Please try to get some rest."

My heart is breaking for her...can hear her crumbling apart on the other end of the line...hate every minute of this charade... don't have any choice but to stick to my plan.

Jake's condition was stabilized. Luckily, the clinic was still closed, and Sofia and Pete were able to work their miracles with no chance of being discovered. Two weeks had passed, and the ploy with Jake's watch and wallet seemed to have worked. The investigators were finalizing their reports, and so far Carlo hadn't heard about any discrepancies. He'd kept his ear to the ground, listening for any issues, but nothing surfaced. It looked like Jake was dead to everyone except four people. His mind jumped from worry about the investigation to concern over Jake's condition, to witnessing Alex's grief. It was much more than most men could shoulder, but he balanced it all as he constructed the next step in his plan.

Pete explained to Carlo that Jake was stable and in an induced coma. He was clear that recovery had no end date. Jake needed time, and he needed to be moved. The clinic's grand opening was scheduled for the first of the month. That gave Carlo time to plan a move. So, that's exactly what Carlo planned, a trans-Atlantic move starting with a call to his brother.

Franco, made a small fortune in his sixty years. He was not only good at making money, but also good at making connections. The *agriturismo* resort Alex and Jake stayed at on their honeymoon was Franco's retirement project. His small empire also expanded to include a luxury resort on Lake Como. He'd purchased the fifteen-hectare, private park along with the main hotel and pavilions. He enjoyed the fruits of his labor running his hospitality business.

With a quick call to his brother in Italy, Carlo explained the urgency of the situation and asked for Franco's help. Carlo made it clear there was a lot at stake. It had to be a clandestine operation, so no one could know who Jake was. It was a lot to ask, but he knew his brother had a big heart and would never say no.

The connections Franco established over the years spanned continents and people, all kinds of people. Some were on the up and up, but others not so much. When he got the call from Carlo, he knew which acquaintances he needed to call.

Franco, like Carlo, believed family came first and loyalty to your friends was right up there in their code of honor. He also wouldn't forget that Jake and Alex had kept their word retaining Carlo and Cara in their jobs at Villa D'Or. Both brothers believed helping Jake was the right thing to do, and neither had given a second thought to their involvement.

Also, Franco had fallen under the spell of Alex's charms when she'd visited his hotel on her honeymoon. They'd kept in touch always talking about another visit to Italy. During their short visit, he'd become fond of Jake and swore to the heavens when Carlo told him about the attack on Jake. So, he was going to do whatever he could do to get Jake to safety and to protect Alex from old man Ricci and his goons.

In a week's time, Franco arranged a private transport for Jake. The air ambulance was staffed by medical air transport specialists, as well as medically configured to service emergencies. Carlo took care of his end along with Sofia and Dr. Pete. On a dark and windy Miami night they moved Jake out of the clinic and onto an isolated Opalocka airstrip west of Miami. The plane sat, engines idling, waiting for their arrival as the medical van pulled up alongside. No one spoke. Everyone moved with precision and within minutes Jake was aboard, and the van was gone.

Carlo knew he couldn't be away from the house for any length of time without raising suspicion, so Sofia went along with Jake for the flight. She hadn't been back to visit her brother, Franco, for a while, so taking a family vacation wouldn't raise any flags.

Franco's resort in the hills of Campania couldn't provide the type of privacy Jake required, but his lake retreat, Villa D' Nord, which for years had been a secret get-a-way to movie stars and princesses, would fit the bill. The main hotel stood on the water's edge with a winding drive that led to the backside portico. Guest arrived under the lofty, stone archway and from there entered the Italian palace which had been converted to a hotel many years before. The suites overlooked the lake, and the park grounds had breathtaking views in every direction. However, as beautiful as they were, they could never provide the privacy needed for a long-term stay, the kind Jake's health required. Franco needed to secure one of the pavilions, and he knew just the one that would work out the best.

The grounds of the resort rose through gardens and pathways to a hilltop crest. The smallest pavilion, a two-bedroom bungalow, sat almost in the woods, tucked away out of sight. Guests requested the large pavilions by the water because of location and size and never ventured near this gem in the trees. This secluded bungalow originally had been assigned to the head gardener, but he'd passed away a year before and his replacement lived nearby with no desire to move his wife to the hotel grounds, so it was empty and far from prying eyes. The entrance door to the compact *casa* faced away from the main resort and was easy to access without being observed. To eliminate any prying eyes, Franco put a reserve notice in the computer and removed the villa from any and all reservations. His chief operations officer didn't ask questions when Franco made it clear that he needed it for his own use for an extended period of time.

Jake was settled in the lodge within two hours of landing at MXP, Milan's Malpensa International Airport. Riding next to Jake, Sofia made sure he was comfortable and medically supervised as they sped along the winding roads to the hotel. The full-time physician and nurse, sworn to secrecy and hired by Franco, met Jake's transport at the door. He was stable, but still in a medically induced coma. The living room had been converted into an ICU, so he could be monitored with a high level of care. This tucked away bungalow perched high over the Italian lake was now home for Jake and would be for quite a while.

Days turned into weeks and weeks into months. Carlo held his breath for each of Franco's calls, fearing the worse and praying for the best. Then there was Alex. Watching her anguish and witnessing her pain was killing him. Hating every minute of the charade, he kept telling himself it was a necessary evil until Jake recovered and could take on the daunting task of going after Ricci for his attempted murder.

Chapter 25
The Reawakening
Aiutati che Dio t'aiuta
(Help yourself and God will help you)

As if an answer to Carlo's prayers, Jake remained stable and slowly came back to the world. The doctor started to see an improvement in his condition, so he gradually reduced the drugs while he monitored Jake's brain activity and vital signs. Jake's recovery was going to be long and hard, but at least he was out of the coma. His breathing had been compromised by the heat of the flames entering his airways, but the swelling had gone down and his breathing was finally stabilized. Once the doctor was able to get the inflammation caused by the burns under control, he started to heal. His brain swelling had reversed, so his prognosis was looking promising.

Tentatively, Jake opened his eyes, and little by little was able to keep them open for more than a few seconds. With a bit of provocation, he responded by wiggling his toes and gripping the doctor's hand. Believing Jake would have recall difficulties, they encouraged his memory by sitting by his side talking to him about Alex and Chris. They played music, told him stories and left the TV on to activate his brain.

Six months passed with Jake responding more and more each day. He finally was able to sit up and eventually began to swallow soft foods. He slowly began to talk again, a few words at a time, then short sentences. Being in such good physical shape before the explosion aided his quick response to therapy. They had him out of bed and walking around the bungalow exercising his weakened legs quicker than expected.

However, the most difficult part came when he started to ask questions. Franco was ready for that. He knew if Jake recovered to the point where he could start making sense of things, he'd look to someone he knew for answers. Not wanting to discuss the particulars in front of the medical team, Franco pulled his car up to the bungalow door and exchanged places with the doctor and the nurse. They'd been cooped up for weeks since their last break and happily agreed to go for a long ride while Franco talked with Jake.

"My friend, you're lucid enough now to realize you are recovering from a terrible ordeal. I'm sure you have questions."

Jake remembered seeing Franco by his bedside, but it all had felt like a dream. Now, Franco was sitting next to him, and it was clear that he was real.

"Franco, what has happened to me? Where am I. Why are you here?"

"You've come a long way, and I don't want to upset you, so you must promise me that you will stay calm, and I promise you I will tell you all that I know."

Jake nodded in agreement and sat back against his pillows to hear the most bizarre story of his life. Franco left nothing out. Piece by piece he unraveled the details of the night of the explosion, and Carlo's part in saving his life. He told him about Sofia and her boyfriend, Dr. Pete, treating him at the clinic and keeping him alive until he could get a medical transport to Italy.

Losing his patience, and no longer able to remain calm, Jake began to raise his voice.

"Why the hell am I in Italy? The doctors in the US could have treated me just as well. What about Alex? Where is she? Why isn't she here? Where's my son? Where's Chris?"

Knowing this was going to be the hardest part to explain, Franco stood up and began to pace in front of the bed.

"Ricci tried to kill you, and he needed to believe he succeeded. My brother made the decision to get you out of the country, believing you could avoid discovery under my supervision better than staying in the States. I have the means to create this hospital environment hidden away on my property, hire your medical team and provide the secrecy and the privacy that couldn't be provided back home."

Jake shook his head in disbelief.

"Why isn't Alex here?"

"That's the other piece of the puzzle, Jake. She thinks you're dead."

"Oh, my God! She what?"

"Carlo overheard you on the phone with Ricci that night. He heard you say something about how dare Ricci bring in your wife and son. You know how fond...no actually, that's the wrong word. You know my brother loves Alex and Chris like they were his own. There was no way he was going to take a chance that Ricci would go after them to get to you. So, he made a quick decision to save your life and protect your wife and son."

What can I say? In all the confusion of the explosion

and with Ricci still on the loose, Carlo did what he thought was best. These brothers saved my life.

Exhausted from the stress of the afternoon, Jake looked Franco in the eye, and promised, "I owe you and your brother a very big debt."

Knowing the total story gave Jake the impetus to fight, and fight he did. He asked Franco to have the furniture removed from the bungalow's living room. In its place Franco filled the space with physical therapy equipment. A treadmill, an elliptical and a rowing machine lined up on one side of the room while weights and balls sat on the other. Most days, Jake fell into bed from both mental and physical exhaustion, but it didn't stop him. He was determined to fight back. The doctor regularly tested his cognition and functional mobility, and as days turned into weeks and months, it was evident that Jake was recovering both mentally and physically. He was thinking clearly now and was slowly formalizing a plan to get back at Ricci without having to jeopardize his family. It was nonstop, excruciating, hard work and intense therapy, but Jake wasn't giving up. He had a wife and child to get home to and a bastard to put in jail. Each morning, he looked in the mirror at the scars that were slowly fading and reminded himself of the family he loved and longed to return to.

Finally feeling stronger, and tired of being cooped up in the villa, one afternoon Jake grabbed a sweater off the chair by the door and headed outside into the fresh air. He was appreciative of all the doctor and nurse had done for him, but was truly sick of their warnings. He was stable enough to go for a walk along the lake and didn't need babysitters.

The last days of summer turned the day into a glorious

display of nature. The dark, blue waters of Italy's deepest lake lapped against the shoreline as the water taxis sped by.

The heat of the afternoon sun feels so good on my back. I can imagine Alex by my side, hand in hand, wandering along the lake, following the curves of the old road, the two of us happy again...I have to make it happen...pretty much fully re-covered...my plan to get Ricci...almost in place. Soon, I'll be on a plane...back to the States...and...my life.

Following Via Regina, Jake wandered through town, turning left toward the water and finding himself in the square at Harry's Bar. The blue of the restaurant's umbrellas matched the blue of the lake and provided protection from the after-noon sun.

I haven't been out in a restaurant since my clandestine arrival at the lake. What can it hurt?

Pulling out a wicker chair, Jake sat back perusing the view.

Remember...Alex...Harry's Bar in Venice. Our honey-moon was so beautiful...her body, so warm...Bellini, that's what Alex ordered there. In honor of Alex and our love, I'm order-ing the same...Whoa...this alcohol is relaxing me...haven't had a drink in so o o long, I feel the buzz...it feels good.

Jake looked at the people gathered at the terrace tables. Already missing Alex beyond measure, watching a couple in love, eyes glued to each other obviously, hungry to return to their hotel room, pained him more. Then, two tourists intently searched a map spread across the table, probably looking for that one last attraction before the end of their vacation. A few tables away, a woman with a huge, straw hat tossed her head back and laughed the most magnetic laugh.

Jake froze. This can't be. I know that laugh. I can't see her face...I don't need to. All this time...sitting a few tables away from my mother-in-law, Valentina.

I don't...know...what...to...do. What is she doing here?
How am I going to get out of here? I can not let her see me.
This is not the way to tell my family I'm alive...if she
turns...even a little...she'll know me. Okay, calm down...get up
slowly...turn my back to her...walk away.

Slide all the lira in my pocket onto the table...pocketed
lira from the kitchen counter before I left for the walk...proba-
bly not enough to cover the bill, but no choice. Quietly push
my chair back...lift myself up...turn at the same time. I can hear
her laugh again...keep moving. I miss Valentina. I miss my
brother, Matt. I miss Alex and Chris. I miss my life.

Heavy heart...make my way back to Franco's bungalow.
The beauty of Lake Como...lost to me...played all the scenar-
ios back and forth...one conclusion.

Pacing the floor, the doctor turned when the door opened.

"Jesus, Jake, I've been looking all over for you. Where have you been?"

"I took a walk to get the hell out of here, Doc. Your face is white. Did you think I died?"

"No, Jake, I didn't think you died. You already missed your chance. I just couldn't imagine you'd take off like that knowing Franco's wishes that you'd stay out of sight."

"Well, I did and I'm glad I did. I almost ran into my mother-in-law. Can you frigging believe that, on my one day out? Luckily, I don't think she saw me. But one thing for sure, today's chance meeting made it very clear to me that it's time to go home. I can't hide forever, and I miss my family. I'm doing well enough now to leave Italy and make my way back to my life."

Chapter 26
The Funeral
Chi si volta, sempre a casa va finire
(No matter where you go, you'll always end up at home)

Seneca Village Limits, another time, it would have been such a welcoming sign. Tonight, it just brought the funeral closer, as well as an unwelcome reminder for Alex that Jake had already been dead a year.

Pulling over, she parked in the lot in front of "Ye Ole Sweet Shop". The shop owner had closed up hours ago. Marking the center of the village, the pristine white spire perched atop the church steeple stood bright against the deep green cluster of Eastern Pines. The familiarity of her hometown wrapped around her like a warm blanket, and she felt safe.

The drive from the airport had given Alex time to sort out her thoughts. Most importantly, she'd found her strength.

My ancestors struggled in so many ways. They left their homes and their families to come to America. They made it possible for me to live my life, and now it's my duty to honor them and to carry on with whatever is put in my path. The dread of Don Ricci's funeral being just a few hours away, the damage he's done with his evil deeds, the pain of losing Jake, none of it is going to break me. I'm not giving up. I know that now. My grandparent's world, my parent's world, my world is sitting next to me with tousled curls and a sweet face. Christopher is the only world that matters.

Just around the bend, the village gazebo marked the history of the settlement. Plaques told the story of this tranquil town that Alex loved so much. Time here seemed to stand still for her. This land had history. The families who settled here had history, and Alex had history. Shaking herself out of her thoughts, she pulled the rental car over and whispered to wake Chris.

"Hey, pumpkin, wake up. I want to show you something."

Chris' soft, sleepy face was scrunched up against his bundled-up sweater. Alex tousled his hair a bit, and his deep brown eyes opened.

"What Mom? I'm so tired."

"Come on, kid. Let's take a short walk. It'll be worth it."

Knowing the funeral would make the next few days grueling, Alex wanted a few quiet minutes to show him the historical plaques and to tell him about the founders' history in her hometown. He loved learning about American history, so she knew it was worth waking him. With a stroll around the park, and Chris now wide awake, they stopped and read each bronze plaque. Knowing Chris' amazing memory, Alex was sure he'd be quizzing his grandmother on the details of the local history by bedtime.

Hungry and eager to get to Valentina's, they headed back to the car and drove a short distance to the house Alex had called home for most of her young life. Hearing the car pull in the driveway, Valentina threw open the back door and rushed down the porch steps. She couldn't contain her excitement to see her daughter and grandson. Throwing her arms around Alex and Chris, she enveloped them as she squeezed them to her.

"Oh, my God. Alexandra, Christopher, you're here. Let me look at both of you."

Her faced beamed love as the last few days of grief faded away. Alex hugged back and kissed her mother's soft cheek. She drank in the smell of Valentina's Norell perfume, and tears of joy filled her eyes. She loved this woman so much and realized just how much she missed her.

Entering the foyer, the warmth of her childhood memories wrapped around her like the comfortable afghans her Aunt Maddy knitted. Everything was the same as if time had stood still. She stopped on the landing, starring at the staircase down to the basement kitchen and the door up to the attic-so many memories running up and down those stairs. Every house has its own smells, and this one smelled like home. She could almost hear the voices drifting through the years, every laugh, every celebration, all those people who shared a life in this house. So many now gone, leaving only the love they'd given and the memories they'd left behind. For a moment, she almost convinced herself she heard her father coming up the stairs. She missed him the most and always would.

"Alexandra, are you going to stand there all night? Come on in, honey."

Valentina's warm voice woke Alex from her sentimental journey.

Chris held his grandmother's hand as she turned to lead them into the kitchen; the family's favorite spot would always be the kitchen.

"So, I made your favorite roast and your favorite chocolate cake and ..."

As Valentina rambled, Alex couldn't help but smile. As much as she knew her mother loved her, Alex always thought Valentina loved Chris more. That was fine with her. She was happy that her son would always know that he was loved beyond measure by plenty of people, especially by his grandmother.

The warmth of home was quickly overshadowed by thoughts of the looming funeral. Alex hated the concept of the Italian funeral. It was exhausting and old fashioned, but thinking about it wasn't going to make a difference. With a deep sigh, she resigned herself to the fact that this was the one tradition that wasn't changing anytime soon.

Looking beautiful in a black dress and black patent leather shoes, Alex tossed her glossy locks over her shoulder and with a deep breath pushed open the glass doors to the funeral parlor. The sweet odor from hundreds of flowers arranged in an assortment of hearts, wreaths and vases surrounded the casket and caught in her throat. The lights were much too bright, and a line of mourners offering condolences was already forming, shaking hands and kissing the cheeks of the Ricci family.

Valentina spotted Alex as she walked through the doors. Knowing her daughter's angst, she rushed over and slipped her arm into Alex's to move her forward into the receiving line.

Phil caught Alex's eye, and a sad smile crossed his tired face. It was evident he was happy she came. He knew what she thought of his father and appreciated her respect for their long history by coming. He nodded thank you to the next person in line, but his thoughts were with Alex. He needed to speak with her. It was not a conversation he could have on the phone. It had to be face to face. If she hadn't come from Miami, he'd already planned to fly south the following week to see her.

"Oh, my God, Alex, you came." He pulled her to him in a bear hug and whispered in her ear, "I missed you and really needed to see your face."

All the anger Alex felt for his father, that had almost kept her from coming, was washed away. She wasn't here for that dead man in the coffin. She was here for her best friend in the whole world, Phil.

"I wouldn't miss it for the world, Phil."

Only Alex could get away with the double entendre. Phil knew her well enough to know that her sarcasm wasn't directed at him. It was just the truth, and they'd always been truthful with each other.

"But, I am sorry for your loss."

Needing to move along in the line, Alex bent over to offer her sympathy to Phil's ninety-year-old aunt, Isabella. She'd also known her all her life. The old lady reached out her feeble hand and pulled Alex close to kiss her cheek. Alex breathed in a subtle hint of moth balls and felt Isabella's thin, cool skin. Aunt Isabella couldn't get up and stand in the line, but she definitely held court from her wheelchair.

"Alexandra, my dear, let me look at you. It's been too long. Thank you for coming all this way."

"I'm sorry for your loss, Aunt Isabella, and I'm sorry it's been so long since I've seen you."

Alex didn't need to say more. The old lady knew what Alex had been through since Jake's death, and she felt terrible for her.

Patting her hand, she whispered, "I understand, my dear girl. I understand."

The only family not present was Andrea. Alex's grandmother's health had failed, so she spent most days quietly resting at home. However, even if she had been healthy enough to attend, it would have been without a great deal of sympathy. Like Alex, she also had nothing good to say about Don Ricci and didn't believe the world would miss him upon his death.

Already exhausted and with no intention of walking up to the casket, Alex turned to walk out of the room, stopping for a moment to take one, last, hard look at Phil's father laying cold in the blue, silk lining of the coffin. Even in death there still seemed to be a smirk on his face. Alex sensed a chill run down her spine at the same time her legs felt wobbly. The pungent odor of flowers hung heavy in the air-lavender mixed with lemon and orange blossom and a heavy note of cedar, sweet like Jade East. The murmured voices from the crowd buzzed in her ears as the room started to spin.

Before she completely collapsed, an arm swooped around her waist, and she felt herself moving toward the door. Once out in the cool air of the vestibule, she focused on Phil's face as he sat her in a huge, silk-brocaded armchair.

"To the rescue again, my princess."

Shaken and confused, Alex pulled herself together.

"Shit, Phil. I almost passed out."

"No kidding. Luckily, I turned around and saw you doing a swan dive. Here's some water. You'll be fine. It was way too hot in there."

Alex took a sip. Her skin was clammy, and her hair was stuck to the back of her neck. The mixed flower scents, just like his cologne, evoked every rotten memory.

That bastard Ricci...for years, living with a haunted

feeling...like something was out of reach...knew I hated him, but never knew how deep...like a word on the tip of the tongue that slips away just as it drifts to consciousness, my memories floated away like distant dreams. Now, I see it all...clearly...his conniving...calculating...controlling moves...on Valentina...on Jake.

Here was the disgusting truth as cold and ugly as the dead body in the next room, along with the frightening realization that memories from the inaccessible corners of her mind were no longer repressed.

Every moment and every scenario from my child-hood...every dinner...nights at the lake...flashing like an old film noir...Jake's death...my poor husband...dead at Ricci's hands...my mother...in Ricci's arms...used us all...I'm glad he's dead.

Shaken, but now calm, she pulled herself together.

Through the maze of hair that had fallen in front of her eyes, she caught two of Mr. Ricci's bodyguards standing at the other side of the foyer, eyes focused on her and Phil.

"I see your father's thugs are still hanging around. What's going to happen to them now, Phil? I hope you're not hiring them to protect you, too."

"Jesus, Alex, you know me better than that. Listen, I have to talk to you, but not here. How long are you staying?"

Phil's face looked super serious. She saw him glance over at Vito, who was nonchalantly moving towards them. She closed her mouth swallowing her words as she stopped short of cracking a joke about Vito being the biggest goon.

"Is everything all right? I mean, other than your father dying?"

"I'm fine. Nothing's wrong. No, actually...Alex, just call me in the morning. It's important. I have to go back in. I'll tell your mother to come get you and head home instead of coming over to the house. It's been a long trip, and you should get some rest."

Alex couldn't imagine why Phil was being so secretive. It wasn't like him to be all mysterious, cloak and dagger was never his style. Already exhausted, she didn't have the strength to question him and this surely wasn't the place to push him for an explanation, so with a thank you for saving her and a kiss on the cheek, she waved him off and promised to call him in the morning.

Chapter 27
The Reunion
Il miglior viaggio ti porta a casa
(The best journey takes you home)

From that serendipitous day in Lake Como at Harry's Bar when Jake was almost discovered alive by Valentina, he'd put his return plan in action. That coincidence was strange luck and definitely the impetus for the realization that he'd been recovering in Italy long enough. He was now physically stronger and there was no reason to stay in Italy, except of course the threat of Ricci still wanting him dead if he found out he wasn't killed in the office explosion.

After being so close to Valentina, Jake couldn't stay away from his family any longer. He also hoped to finalize his original plan to expose Ricci's financial scheme, so he told Carlo that he was coming home and asked for his assistance in booking a flight from Milan direct to Miami.

All those months, he'd never taken a ride on the lake, and wanting to say thank you to Franco, he thought a boat ride might be a nice way to say a proper good bye. So, Jake booked a private boat along with an Italian lunch for the afternoon and asked Franco to meet him at the boat dock. Jake owed his life to Franco and to Carlo. He'd thank Carlo when he got home, but now he'd say his thanks to Franco. The blue of the sky couldn't have been bluer that day. Gorgeous pink and purple bougainvillea, rooting along the shore, exploded with color along the winding stretch of the lake. Jake was saddened that he hadn't been able to enjoy this beautiful place with Alex, but he promised himself he'd bring her back to Italy as soon as he could.

Life-changing events have a way of bringing people together, and friends become family. Franco was now family to Jake and Jake was family to Franco. Jake put his arm around his dear friend.

"I don't know how I can ever repay you. I am indebted to you for the rest of my life."

"You can repay me by going home to your wife and son, living a good life and finally getting that Ricci bastard."

They promised to keep in touch and to visit. Franco worried about what Jake was returning to and begged him to stay alert and to rely on Carlo. With heartfelt hugs, these two men whose lives had been so intertwined, said their goodbyes.

Carlo had been talking to Jake ever since Jake saw Valentina that day at the lake bar. Now that Jake was healthy and also adamant about returning to the States, Carlo had no choice but to follow Jake's lead. He'd made a very difficult decision to fake Jake's death, and Jake had every right to plan his return.

Carlo made his clandestine calls to Jake in Italy away from Alex and Villa D'Oro. Carlo and Jake raked over the details, and both agreed there was no right way to tell Alex that Jake was alive. One point they totally agreed on was that they needed to keep Jake's return a secret from Ricci. No matter what, Jake needed time to set Ricci up for the fall. He couldn't do it from Italy, but he could do it from the confines of Villa D'Oro.

George, the driver Ricci had assigned to Jake, had long been removed from his job. Alex saw to it that anyone that had anything to do with Ricci was kept far away from her family. Carlo's wife, Cara, had been keeping Jake's secret for a year, and was in no way going to jeopardize his return, so the only concern was Mrs. Hermes. Carlo's plan was to suggest to Alex that Mrs. Hermes hadn't taken a vacation in a while and had been talking about visiting her sister in Haiti. If he could get her out of the house, no one would be there to accidentally expose Jake's return. It would give Jake time to put his plan against Ricci to work. By the time Mrs. Hermes returned, everyone would know Jake was alive.

There was no right way to tell Alex, but they both decided the best way would be for Carlo to ask her to join him in the garden. It was the end of the season for her knock-out roses, and the hedges were struggling with an infestation. Carlo knew if he asked her to take a look, she'd not refuse. Once in the garden, under the blue Miami sky, he'd find a way to tell her Jake was alive and coming home.

Jake's flight home across the pond was the usual nine hours, but this flight felt like forever. Landing at MIA, he knew Carlo would be there to pick him up and to help him ease back into his life with Alex and to achieve his objective with Ricci. He never expected what he heard when he got into Carlo's car.

"Dead? He's dead? Jesus, Carlo. He's dead?"

Jake couldn't believe his ears. Old man Ricci had died.

"Yes, he died. I tried to reach you in Italy, but my calls

wouldn't go through. You know service can be spotty on those Italian lakes."

"We had a severe windstorm which completely knocked out the lines. Obviously, if you couldn't reach me, service is still down."

"No, I got through to Franco after your plane took off. The service was back on, but you were already in the air. Believe me, if I could have reached you, I would have. I also wanted to tell you that Alex wasn't home. Chris flew with her to New York."

"New York?"

"Yes, they went to Seneca. Alex arranged to go to the funeral, but she also took Chris, so he could spend some time with Valentina and the family. Mrs. Hermes left as planned for Port Au Prince this morning. In fact, I dropped her to MIA before I picked you up. So, it's just Cara and me until Alex and Chris get back."

Ricci was dead, but Jake had never seen which thug Ricci had sent that night to kill him. Luckily, Carlo saw Vito running out of the building. So, the putting Ricci down part of the plan was over, but Jake knew he still had to expose Ricci's scheme and above all get the guy who left him for dead in the fire.

"Jake, Alex and Chris will be home in a few days. How about using the time to get reacquainted with your life here at Villa D'Oro?"

Jake knew he had to wait. His return had to be delicately handled with Alex, and especially with Chris. "It sounds like a plan, Carlo. I was hoping to hold my family in my arms tonight, but I have no choice but to wait a few more days."

Alex was ready to go home. The funeral exhausted and

unnerved her, but after seeing Chris so happy with his cousin, she knew it was time to put this chapter in their lives behind them and to focus on her son.

Phil's admission by the lake front of the truth about Jake's death just added to the weight she was carrying on her shoulders. She felt terrible for Phil. What a horrible thing for him to know that his father had killed Jake.

Tearful goodbyes filled the airport waiting area as Valentina hugged her daughter and squeezed Chris to her breast. Every time they left Seneca, Valentina's heart broke as she stood at the airport's glass wall waving at their plane wishing them a safe trip.

Alex and Chris's flight was uneventful, and they landed at MIA right on time. Carlo waiting at the luggage turnstile, greeted them with a welcoming smile as he whisked their bags to the car. They made small talk on the way home, discussing how long Mrs. Hermes would be gone and what Cara should make for dinner. Nothing of importance, but Alex could sense something wasn't right. Carlo seemed uptight and too jovial at the same time. Then, before they pulled into the driveway, he asked her if she would take a look at the rose garden. He said something about an issue with aphids. Her first response was she was too tired and would look later, but then, seeing his eyes in the rear-view mirror, something told her she needed to say yes.

"Sure, Carlo, Chris can get his swim trunks in the pool house and take a swim. The rose garden is within sight of the pool, so I can look at the rose issue and keep an eye on Chris at the same time."

Trying to hide his anxiety, Carlo joked.

"Wonderful, roses and swimming come first. The luggage can wait. I'll bring it in later."

Carlo had hoped she'd come to the garden, so he was ready, as ready as he could ever be, to break the news. Jake was waiting upstairs in his library pacing the floor, wanting to tell them himself, but not wanting to frighten them, so he waited while Carlo softened the blow.

Leading Alex to the old, stone bench, he motioned for her to sit across from the roses.

"Alex, you've been through a great deal in the last year, so much more than any young woman should have to go through. Can you only imagine if things were different? If things were not what you thought they were? If there was a different ending to your story?"

"Carlo, what is going on? What are you talking about?"

Alex had never seen Carlo act so strangely.

"It's obvious you are trying to tell me something, so please say what you need to say."

Seeing her frustration building, Carlo rushed his words.

"I'm trying to tell you that everything is going to be ok. I'm so sorry to have kept this from you all this time, but it was for the best. Ricci tried to kill Jake in that fire, but he didn't succeed."

Before Alex could respond, her eyes followed her son as he scrambled out of the pool, running and yelling.

"Daddy, Daddy!"

My dad...what...he never died...something bad happened...he's not dead. Someone made my dad go away for a long time. His eyes are tired... so tired. Something is different. What happened to his face? Mmm...his hug is the same. Mom... now...she'll be happy. She's been so sad. We made it... we're not alone... a family again.

Now, the catch in Carlo's voice matched the tears streaming down Alex's cheeks.

Jake. My love. This has to be a dream

"Yes, Alex, he's alive, and he's come home to you."

Jake swooped Christopher into the air and swung him above his head.

"Hey, kiddo, it's so good to see you."

He hugged his son to his chest as he moved forward toward Alex.

A dream...

Never a loss for words, Alex couldn't utter a sound.

My love, Jake...oh my god... I can't breathe. My knees are shaking...I can't move my feet. Jake is holding Chris...he's moving toward me...I'm not dreaming, can't be real... I'm not dreaming.

It was like one of her slow, moving dreams, only this time she knew she was awake. Seeing her response, Carlo came up behind her and gently put his hand on her back.

"It's ok, Alex. It's a long story, but he's home again. Go to him."

Carlos' words woke her from her daze and gave her the strength to move. Now she was running up the path and Jake was running toward her. He put Chris down and pulled her into his arms. Tears were pouring mixed with laughter and squeals. Carlo stayed back, letting the family bond. He couldn't have been a happier man. All was right with the world.

The revelry in the garden moved to the house. Expecting a family reunion, Cara prepared a sumptuous feast and set the dining room table. It was the celebration of a lifetime. Everyone talked at once. There was so much to say and so much to explain. Chris' questions were the easiest to satisfy. Jake told him he'd been sick far away in a hospital and hadn't been able to call home. That's all his young mind needed-at least that's what Jake hoped. The explanation was good enough for Chris because his dad was home, and that's all that mattered.

Once dinner was over and an exhausted Chris was tucked into bed, Carlo and Cara left Alex and Jake to their privacy. They couldn't have been happier if they were welcoming their own son home.

Hand in hand, Alex and Jake silently walked down the path to the water's edge and snuggled in each other's arms on one large chaise and watched the day's light fade away. They'd have time to talk tomorrow. Tonight was for holding each other and just knowing they were together again was enough.

The following morning, Cara was back in the kitchen bright and early. So joyful to be part of the reunion, she hummed her way through her kitchen chores. Not wanting Chris away from them and concerned he could divulge his father's secret return to someone at school, they opted to keep him home until things were safe. Giving Jake the time he needed to talk with Alex, Carlo took Chris outside and spent the morning tossing balls and playing games in the yard.

Finally, tucked away in the library together, Alex had her turn for questions. Jake relayed his story, starting out by saying they still needed to be careful.

"Alex, when Carlo was waiting in the office garage that night, he saw Ricci's guy, Vito, leave the building. I never saw who hit me, but logic says it was him. He took the files that proved there was a scam going on and left me for dead. Even though old man Ricci is dead, it doesn't make it safe for me or for you and Chris. If Vito finds out I'm alive, he will assume I can identify him and that makes him a very dangerous man."

"What are we supposed to do, Jake? You can't hide forever."

"No, Alex, I can't. This is only going to be for a short time, just until I can gather proof again of Ricci's scam and finger Vito for my attempted murder. Let's just lie low here at the house until I get things worked out."

"Aren't we going to tell my mother? My God, we can't keep this from her, Jake."

"Right now, the fewer people who know I'm alive, the better. However, I am planning to enlist Phil's help. If what you say is true, his confession about his father's guilt shows he'll be willing to help. Hopefully, he can help me put the case together to prove his father attempted to have me killed to keep me quiet. Once we have solid proof, I can have the police take over, and they can go after Vito. In the meantime, we should be very careful and act like nothing has changed. I'll stay out of sight, and you can go about your life as you were doing before. We just need some time, and this will all be over soon."

How can I argue with Jake's plan? There is no sense in taking a chance that Vito will go after Jake again. Plus, I know we'll have Phil's help. He was so sick over what his father did, I'm sure he'll give Jake all the assistance he needs to nail Vito.

Excited to tell Phil that Jake was alive, they decided to call him immediately. Alex made the call and Phil answered.

"Alex, how's my girl? Was it a good flight home? Thanks again for coming north to the funeral. I know it wasn't easy for you, but I want you to know how much it means to me that you did. By the way, I'm moving my schedule up for the Miami office. It looks like I'll be coming down next week to get the ball rolling."

Alex smiled at Phil's plan.

"It's a great idea, Phil. In fact, I know someone who can help you get that office up and running again."

"You do? Who?"

"Jake."

Before Phillip could respond, Alex turned the phone

over to Jake.

"Hey, old buddy. How's life been treating you?"

There was dead silence on the other end of the line.

"Sorry if I shocked you, Phil."

Jake could only imagine how happy his good friend was to hear his voice.

"You there, Phil? Yup, it's me come back from the dead."

"Jesus Christ, Jake, is that really you?"

"Sure is, my friend. Do I have a story to tell you? You won't believe the year I've had. But first, I'm back home in Miami with the love of my life, and I'm healthy enough to go after the bastard who tried to kill me."

"Jesus, Jake, didn't Alex tell you it was my father? He found out you were going to expose his scam and wanted you out of the picture."

"Yes, she told me. It takes a big man to admit his father would do something like that, Phil. I appreciate your honesty and can't thank you enough for being there for my wife. But your father only gave the order. It was Vito who did the deed."

"Vito? What makes you think it was Vito?"

"Carlo was waiting for me in the parking garage and saw Vito leave the office building just before the explosion. There's no question that he was doing your father's dirty business. So, besides calling to say hello, I'm alive, I'm also calling to enlist your help. I need to get proof again that there was a scam worth keeping me quiet, and then I can turn the information over to the police, along with Vito. All the proof I had was taken the night Vito knocked me out and started the fire. Now, I need to lie low, so we're not telling anyone I'm alive, except you. Not my brother, Matt, not anyone until this is over. Will you help me expose the truth?"

Phil, still trying to wrap his head around the fact that his friend was alive, answered quickly.

"Sure, Jake. I'll help you. Absolutely will. You know, the fire badly damaged the Miami office, and it's still under renovation. Besides, I doubt there's much incriminating evidence left. Like you said, your flash drive was taken that night. But there's a ton of information in my father's New York office. Why don't you come up here? You can stay with me and no one will know you're here. I'll collect whatever you need from the office and funnel it to you. You just tell me what to look for, and I'll do it. Besides, it will be great to see you again, buddy."

Jake fell silent.

"Jake, are you there?"

"Oh, yes, yes, Phil, I'm here. I was just thinking that I just got home after more than a year away, and I hate to leave Alex and Chris so soon. But it makes sense. If the fire destroyed evidence in the office here, then I'll have to come north. I want to move on with my life, I've got to get this done and done quickly. Thanks for offering to help me out. I'll catch the next flight out."

"Perfect. Actually, I was planning to go out to the lake. Summer's over and there's no one out there this time of year, so you'd be safe away from prying eyes. Why not plan on spending the weekend with me there? We can do a bit of fishing and go over our attack strategy and be ready to hit the road running Monday morning. You'll get the proof you need."

Jake couldn't wait for all of this to be over. Fingers crossed, he'd soon be able to go back to his life without living in fear.

"Sounds like a plan. I'll let you know which flight I'm on, my friend. I'll see you soon."

Alex didn't want to see Jake go away again, but she agreed there was no way he was going to find any proof in the burned-out Miami office. She wanted him to get whatever information he could get out of the New York office and put the puzzle together from there. If she could hang on a little longer, this nightmare would finally come to an end. Knowing she was going to miss him more than ever, she didn't leave his side and wouldn't take no for an answer, jumping in the car with him for his ride to the airport.

But, what Alex didn't know was that Jake's objective had quickly changed. To protect her, there was no way he could tell her what he was planning to do.

Chapter 28
The Sting
Perché ho un fratello ho sempre un amico
(Because I have a brother I always have a friend)

After Jake's reported death, Alex and Jake's brother, Matt, had taken turns calling each other. Alex knew Matt was checking in on her and Chris out of brotherly love, and she truly relied on her contact with him. He recognized she was struggling with his brother's death and wanted to offer all the support he could. He was devastated, but never showed it in front of Alex. He couldn't be much support to her if he fell apart and displayed his grief, so he became a strong shoulder for Alex to cry on.

Luckily, when Jake was in graduate school in Cambridge, Alex had gotten to know Matt. At the time, he was still living in the old neighborhood and was attending the police academy. He wasn't far from Cambridge, so they spent many a night together in the local pubs. He was a good guy, and she'd taken an immediate liking to him. In fact, she didn't know until after their first few beers together that Matt was also working at the Killington ski slope that lucky day she met Jake and had seen her take the ugly, mogul run.

Gentrification of their old neighborhood had started while Jake and Alex were living in Cambridge, and Matt wanted to be part of it. The first chance he got, he bought the multi-family house where they'd grown up in Charlestown. By then, Mr. and Mrs. Kelly had moved to an assisted living facility and the twin's family had moved out to the suburbs. The only Murphy who stayed was Ella Murphy. Matt married one of the twins they'd grown up with. Not Jake's first love, Emma, but her sister, Ella.

With Jake gone, Matt was lost. He was, a man of the law, and he couldn't even protect his own brother. He always believed things would have ended differently if Jake had let him in on the Ricci scam he'd been investigating. Being a tough guy was never Jake's forte. Dealing with tough guys was more Matt's style.

Once Carlo dropped Jake off at the Miami airport and Alex stopped hugging him goodbye, Jake rushed to the ticket counter hoping to get a standby seat. He was looking forward to seeing his old friend and to getting this mess over with.

Alex was sad he had to leave, so when she returned home, she kept herself busy in the garden room trying to pass time when the phone rang, She saw the caller ID. It was Matt. She didn't know what to do. At first, she wasn't going to answer. It would be easier to say nothing than to lie to him. But how could she not tell Matt? There was nothing he would do that would jeopardize Jake's plan. He didn't even live in New York.

Alex picked up the phone.

"Alex, it's Matt. How are you and Chris doing? Ella and I miss you both."

Alex was bursting with the good news. She had to tell someone that Jake was alive. Blurting out the whole story, she left Matt stunned on the other end of the line.

"My brother is alive! Oh my God, Alex. He's alive. I can't believe this. But wait a minute. Are you telling me that Jake is going after this Vito on his own? Didn't he learn the first time that these people are dangerous?"

"He's not alone, Matt. Phil offered to help Jake put a case together to expose everything and everyone. In fact, Jake already flew to New York. He left Miami a few hours ago and should be landing at JFK soon. He's connecting there to a flight to the Syracuse. Phil offered to pick him up, and he's going to spend the weekend doing some fishing at Phil's summer house on the lake. By Monday, they'll have a plan together to expose old man Ricci's scheme and turn Vito into the authorities."

"That's great, Alex. It's good to know that Jake has it all under control. I can't wait to see him. I just can't believe he's alive."

Matt had a call coming through and apologized for getting off the phone.

"Sorry, Alex, gotta take this call. Give Chris a hug from me. Talk soon."

It was strange for Matt to rush off the phone like that, but Alex guessed he was just shocked to hear the news of Jake's return and needed some time to digest it all.

That call coming in was Jake. The caller ID lit up, Unknown Caller, so Matt didn't get off the phone with Alex because he had to take an important call. He got off the phone because he was going to leave for the lake to help Jake. He couldn't believe his brother was going after these people and Vito again without his help. Was he trying to get himself killed a second time? But, it turned out, the Unknown Caller was

Jake. And Jake had a plan.

Jake landed at the Syracuse airport, and just as promised, Phil was there waiting for him at the baggage claim. Jake insisted they stop for dinner in Bridgeport at one of their favorite diners before driving out to the lake. In celebration, Jake ordered two of their famous hamburger platters and told the bartender to stack up shots and to keep them coming.

"Hey, everybody, tonight is a great celebration."

A few of the bar patrons turned to see what he was talking about.

Putting his arm around Phil, "This my dear people is my buddy. I just came back from the dead, and I couldn't be happier to be back, and I know he couldn't be happier for me, so drinks all around." Jake raised his glass, "To my good friend Phil who stood by my wife while I was dead."

Free booze in a neighborhood bar never being refused, the people in the bar raised their newly filled glasses and joined the toast. When they finally got back in the car, Phil talked on and on about how they were going to get Vito and expose his father. Jake seemed to be tipsy and kept pretty much quiet for the whole ride, until they approached a Save More Now convenience store.

"Phil, would you mind pulling over? I need to get a few things. I might as well get them now, so I don't have to go back out."

Phil, was anxious to get to the lake, but he pulled into the parking lot.

"I'll be just a minute. Be right out."

Inside, Jake walked to the back of the store and hit redial on his cell. Grabbing some Tylenol and a bottle of water, he paid and headed back out to the waiting car.

"You get what you needed?"

"Yeah, I get headaches since the attack, so I bought some Tylenol."

"Jake, why didn't you ask me. I've got all kinds of meds at the lake house?"

"I didn't think, no problem. It's better I have a big bottle in my pocket in case I get one my wicked migraines."

"Shit, man. I'm so sorry this happened to you. A nice long weekend at the lake will do you good."

The flight to JFK and the connecting flight to Syracuse total at least four to five hours, and the drive from the airport to the lake is another thirty to forty minutes. The drive from Boston to the lake could take about the same amount of time, depending on how fast Matt drove. Jake needed to stall as much as he could, so the diner stop and med stop gave him some of the precious time he needed.

Once out of the car, Phil headed straight for the house. Musty from lack of use, he opened the windows and lowered the AC to circulate the air. Checking the refrigerator, he groaned.

"Damn it. I told the housekeeper to stock this fridge. I swear she's fired this time!"

"Don't worry about it, Phil. I can always go back out and get supplies. I'm going to head down to the boathouse and take a look at the lake. It's been a long time, since I've enjoyed that view."

Once outside, Jake hit redial again. Not wanting to be caught on the phone, he didn't say a word. The call was his signal. With the phone on silent, a reply call vibrated his phone once and then hung up.

Standing in the boat house, staring at the lake, brought back a world of memories. So many nights on this lake front watching the sunset, laughing with Alex and his best friend, Phil.

Interrupting the night's stillness, a faint shuffle in the gravel alerted Jake. Before he could turn around, Phil's voice, low and strangely sinister, floated through the boathouse.

"You know Jake, Mohawk Lake being relatively shallow can be treacherous to boaters, especially at night. It's so easy for a speedboat going at high speed to hit a hazardous shoal, and for the driver or even a passenger to hit his head while going overboard and subsequently drown."

Jake turned to face Phil, who was standing in the darkened boathouse with a gun aimed at Jake's chest.

"Phillip, what are you saying? Jesus, Phil...a gun? What are you doing with that gun? What's going on? You're my best friend. Why are you aiming a gun at me?"

"You really are stupid, Mister Harvard Smart Ass. Your best friend? You've been nothing but a pain in my ass since I met you. Actually, since Alex met you. I had it all planned. She'd come home from college, and she'd be mine. Yes, mine, like she'd been our whole childhood. But then you came along. "Jake...this" and "Jake...that", that's all I heard from her. It made me sick. But there wasn't anything I could do, but bide my time.

So, when my father hired you against my wishes, I made him move you to the Miami office. Big Jake exiled. I needed you out of New York, so you wouldn't stick your nose in my business. All those long weekend visits I made to Villa D'Oro, that was me needing to see Alex, not you.

The scam you uncovered in Miami was my father's brainchild. He thought you'd never discover his scheme, since he kept you on a short lease in that office. But of course, being a goody, goody two-shoes, you had to stick your nose in our business, and look what happened."

Jake's suspicion had become a reality.

"Dear God... are you telling me... it was you all this time, Phil?"

"Actually, you finding out about the scam and threatening to turn my father in... oh, by the way, that was me on the phone that night. Everyone always said my father and I sounded alike on the phone. Remember, you kept saying, 'I can't hear you.' Well, genius, that was me intentionally causing a bad connection, making sure my voice was camouflaged enough for you to think it was my father. As I was saying, your investigation actually sped up my plan to get rid of you and make Alex mine."

"Phil, please don't tell me that was you, not Vito, that night in the office."

"No, Vito is my man, always has been. He does what I tell him to do. I told him to get those damn files, actually your clever little flash drives, and to get rid of you. Yes, sorry old boy, my father had nothing to do with your death. It was me. He may have been a bastard, but he wasn't your murderer."

With you out of the picture, I was biding my time to make a move on Alex. I know she's always loved me, at least until you came into the picture. And my plan was working. I already buttered her up with my father's fake deathbed confession. She's feeling so sorry for me and loves me even more because I was so honest with her. And now I'm moving to Miami to be closer to her. It won't be long before she'll realize we belong together. I'll make sure of that. I dream about hold-ing her in my arms. Just thinking about her makes me hard. Soon, my dear boy, that will be a realty."

Jake clenched his fists, concentrating on Phil's face and his bizarre statement about Alex. It took all his strength not to lung forward and punch Phil's face out. But he knew to stay cool.

"No more talking, Jake, get in the boat. We're going for a ride. Sorry to say, I'm the only one coming back. Like I said before, this can be a treacherous lake at night."

Matt hung up on Alex, but not because he was in shock. He needed to get to the lake before anything else happened to his brother. He was going without being asked. Then he answered Jake's phone call. His brother needed his help. Matt knew if he used his siren and rushed like hell, he could make it there in time. Grabbing his gear and a thermos of black coffee, he jumped in his car and headed west. Figuring Jake's ETA at the Syracuse airport along with drive time to the lake, he should arrive not too much after Jake and Phil. He just needed Jake to stall as much as he could, go to dinner-anything to give him enough time to get there.

Phil detected Jake's focus shift over his left shoulder. As he turned, he realized they were not alone.

"Don't move, Phil. Put the gun down. The only one not coming back here is you. I heard everything you said, and re-member, asshole, I'm a cop. Sorry, but you won't be taking my brother out to the middle of that lake tonight. You're not killing him a second time. Phillip Ricci you're under arrest for your

Ponzi scheme and for the attempted murder of my brother. You have the right to remain silent. Anything you say..."

Jake let out a deep sigh. He'd been blind. All these years he never knew Phil had such a sick crush on Alex. Sick enough to kill him and let her grieve for a year until he could butter her up and make a move on her. Jake's stomach turned at the thought of this twisted bastard going near his wife.

He'd been oblivious until today. Phil gave it away on the phone. Jake never said flash drive. He never told anyone the incriminating information he'd collected was transferred to a flash drive. He'd had no reason to be so specific. All he'd ever described were files. He hadn't shared that information with Franco the year he was recovering in Italy. Once home in Miami, he'd never used that term talking to Alex or Carlo. How did Phil know it was a flash drive? There was only one way Phil could have known the evidence was on a flash drive.

Putting the pieces together, Jake made the call to his brother before he stepped on the plane. He really hoped Phil would prove him wrong, but he wasn't taking any chances. If his suspicion was correct about Phil, he would need a witness and hefty back up.

Matt threw his arms around his brother.

"Jesus, man. It's great to see you. You are a site for sore eyes!"

Phil struggled in his handcuffs as his shrieks reverberated across the lake.

"I'll get out of this. I didn't do a thing. I didn't try to kill you. It was Vito. Matt is your brother. He'd lie for you. You have no proof."

"Shut up, Phil. Is this proof enough?"

Matt hit play on his cell phone's record button, and Phil's voice echoed in the boat house and into the dark night.

Epilogue

Two Shores
La vita torna al punto di partenza
(Life comes full circle)

"Ladies and gentlemen, please fasten your seatbelts. We'll be landing shortly in Naples. On behalf of myself, our flight crew and all of us at Alitalia, we thank you for flying with us and hope to see you again soon. Welcome to Italy."

Italy, it was music to Alex's ears.

Another year had gone by, but this one was a better year for Alex D'Amato Reed. Jake was alive and had come back to her. Ricci Financials no longer existed. Once investigated, Jake was acquitted of any wrongdoing. He'd been proven innocent and shamefully clueless in the whole affair. On the other hand, three of Ricci's plants and the Ricci father-and-son team, were proven to be expert schemers. Old man Ricci beat the system by dying before the law could catch him, but for his life's work he'd left a tarnished legacy behind. Michael Foster and Sammy Leon from the Miami office went down hard. In total, some involved were smart and talented men, others just slick, shady opportunists. However, they all went down for the same trouble and the same desire, greed.

Her family was once again safe with Vito in prison serving a life sentence on an attempted murder charge for assaulting Jake and leaving him for dead, as well as a murder charge for killing Charlie, the custodian, in the process. Phil was no longer a concern. He'd been put away, too. He'd gone absolutely bonkers once he was turned in to the authorities. Not going easily, he'd grabbed for one of the cop's guns and tried to run. Those antics just added to the long list of charges against him.

It had taken Alex months to digest the truth about Phil. His deception had been tremendously difficult for her to accept. She demanded to hear the recording Matt made in the boathouse, so any time she doubted the truth, she'd replay Phil's words in her head. It was the one thing that helped her put his betrayal behind her, so she could move on with her life.

Seeing Ricci dead in his coffin and knowing Jake was alive gave Alex the permission she needed to end her life-long hatred of Ricci and her year of grieving. Little by little, she started to feel more like her carefree self again. With her loving husband and her amazing son by her side, she knew she'd be able to deal with the truth and truly bury both Riccis.

At almost 100 years old, Andrea let time take its toll. She accepted her fate, and said goodbye to this world. She'd made good choices in her life and more than anything knew together with Giu's love, she'd touched humanity through her amazing granddaughter, Alexandra.

Valentina, grieving her mother's passing and wanting to stay close to her daughter and her grandson, moved to Miami and was welcomed at Villa D'Oro. The house had plenty of space for family, and it was time for them to bond the generations.

Christopher was content. His dad was home and his parents were together again. Even better, the house was always full of visiting family from Seneca. He had his Nanna to fuss over him, too. Many a morning she'd scoot Cara or Mrs. Hermes out of the kitchen and take over the breakfast preparation, especially just for him.

Carlo also couldn't believe his good luck. From the first day he saw Cara in that convent garden in the Italian countryside to the gardens of Villa D'Oro, fate had blessed him, and he had always done his best to give back and act in good faith.

Alex had much to be thankful for. She'd suffered a great deal, but everything had finally come together in her world. Glancing at Chris and Jake, she beamed and flashed that Alex smile. The two most important people in her life were sitting in the seats next to her.

Jake's voice broke into the pilot's announcement.

"Hey, buddy, looks like we'll be landing soon. Let's get our seats upright. Are you excited to see Italy for the first time?"

"For sure, Dad. I can't wait to try real Italian pizza."

They were going back to where it all had started for Alex's ancestors and to the people who spent a year bringing her husband back to life.

It was time to rejoice as a family and introduce Christopher to his Italian roots.

As the plane's wheels touched the runway on Italian soil, a sweet smile spread across Alex's face. Turning to Jake and Chris, her eyes sparkled with love.